Canadian Cataloguing in Publication Data
A. Tarrant
Playing With Shadows
978-1-895166-46-0
1. Fiction. I. Title.
Printed and bound in North America.
First published in 2023
by Inconsequential Diversions

PLAYING
WITH SHADOWS

A. Tarrant

Stage Direction for the theatrical version of *Playing With Shadows*.

This video segment—from George Attwell's interview on a national television news show—should be projected onto the screen at the back of the stage.

George Attwell

Lawrence, Cornwallis, Monckton. Some call it ethnic cleansing … what happened with the Acadians I mean … even genocide … but they were heroes all.

Buddy Leblanc

So, can we go back to that afternoon? You went to the Maclean-Dill Building?

George Attwell

Yeah, cus it gives a good view of the park where the snowflakes were doing their latest bit to destroy our heritage. The east sidewalk starts at the centre of the park and runs all the way to the street, right across the road from the Maclean-Dill Building. Four stories up and you got a perfect view.

Buddy Leblanc

Of the circle in the centre of the park?

George Attwell

Yeah. Sniper's dream. Where that Black broad was spewing all her shit about how everyone is racist and you gotta tear down statues and rename stuff to make it politically correct. I'd had enough. Ever since I got out of the military it'd been one protest after the other. Sickening.

Buddy Leblanc

In this case the protest was regarding the fact that the park is named after a man who was part of Belgium King Leopold's genocide in the Congo.

George Attwell

So you call it. There was lots of disease and private companies got carried away a few times. That's all. The name of the park was fine till all these immigrants came over here and instead of becoming Canadians decided to stir up shit. They wanna change everything to suit them; to make Canada like their shithole countries. Trump was right.

Buddy Leblanc

Tanya Thomas was born in Halifax. ... In any case, do you remember what time you got to the Maclean-Dill Building?

George Attwell

Yeah. 2:00 o'clock.

Buddy Leblanc

And what happened then? Can you walk me through your movements.

George Attwell

Well I had my dark blue sports bag with me. I go in and there's no guard on duty at the reception desk. That's why I went at the time I did. I watched the place for a couple of days and saw he does his rounds about then. At 2:00, like I said.

I'm wearing my shades and a black hoodie with the hood up, and a baseball cap underneath with the brim sticking out to hide my face from the security camera. I look down at the floor when I walk under it. The security's another thing I checked out before—where the cameras are—and I only seen the one.

So I avoid the elevator and take the stairs. I can hear voices through the stairwell door on the second floor and they're coming down the hall. So I boot it up the next flight and then stop. But the voices go by and then get fainter so I climb the rest of the stairs to the fourth floor.

I know about the empty office facing the park. The door's unlocked. I go in and crank open the window. You know the type (makes cranking motion with hand). … It's an old building.

I watch the mouthy broad with the megaphone for a bit and get all pissed off. I hate these traitors. They attack our white history; our white English heritage that made this country. They attack men like Charles Lawrence who did what had to be done. The Acadians had to go. They and the Indians couldn't be trusted.

So's I get all pissed off watching this bitch cus our history has to be respected. Monuments and street and park names must stand to remind all of who we are—Nova Scotians.

I remember that this country can only be taken back by its rightful white, Anglo, Christian owners … with violence. It's time for a revolution. A race war. And it's down to me to kick it off.

So, after thinking about all this stuff again, I get all worked up and it's easy to do what I have to; to do what I'm there for. I take my tripod outta the sports bag and unfold it. Then I assemble the .308 with its scope. I practised this a bunch of times so I can do it with my eyes closed. Once I get the rifle assembled I put it on the tripod and stick its barrel through the open window. I take off my shades and aim.
The shot's fuckin' deafening but it's perfect.

Buddy Leblanc

You shot Tanya Thomas.

George Attwell

Yeah, the mouthy Black troublemaker. Uniacke Square trash.

Buddy Leblanc

And what did you do then?

George Attwell

Well I see the broad go flying and I'm a long way away but I hear all the screaming and shouting. Everybody's diving for cover, even the cop who's there. But I'm an ice cube. I fire off a few more rounds—for effect like—then pack things up. I just walk down the stairs and out of the building.

Buddy Leblanc

Did you see anybody on your way out?

George Attwell

Not a soul and there's nothing to hear. People probably heard the shot and froze like.
But it's not silent. There's traffic and noise

out on the sidewalk. I can hear sirens.
But you know I'm not thinking about the
stuff going on around me. I'm thinking
about my daughter back in Alberta. I know
that that night there'll be a massive bonfire
and a huge pot of boiling water and corn on
the cob, and my daughter will be there, and
she'll think of me and know I'm not a
coward, and know that I'd do anything to
give her a better world than the one I grew
up in.

Buddy Leblanc
What can you tell me about the people who
supported you in the killing?

George Attwell
No, no, no. Nothing. I acted alone.

Thursday. My name is Peter Russell. I live in Halifax, Nova Scotia. I'm an actor. I create shadows.

I positioned my laptop so the camera wouldn't capture my hands—which I thought might be shaking—as I auditioned online for the role of Conor in an upcoming film.

It was a period piece. A Romeo and Juliet story about a Catholic woman and a Protestant man set in Saint John, New Brunswick in 1849.

The resident Irish Protestants saw the newly arrived Irish Catholics, fleeing the potato famine, as inferiors and outsiders. Immigrants out to steal their jobs.

The Protestant man, Conor, has been knocked senseless during the July 12th parade, provocatively run through the Catholic part of town.

To save his life, the Catholic woman, Biddy, has pulled him into her house.

> **Cut to**: **Conor** is still looking dazed, but is sitting up on the floor. **Biddy** finishes unwrapping a bandage wound around his forehead.

> **Conor**
> If I leave and try to walk down the street I may not survive.

> **Biddy**
> And you won't survive if you stay here when my father and brothers return. There's a back door. The privy is at the back of the yard with a shelter for wood beside it. Lay behind that, out of sight, and wait for dark. (Stands up.) We must go!

Cut to: **Conor** getting up with help, shakily. **Biddy** then lets go of him, bends, picks up the wrapping cloth and wipes the blood from the floor.

Cut to: **Conor** being assisted through the **backyard** by **Biddy**. In the background, muffled since coming from outside, we can once again hear **noises** from the July 12th march, now in the distance: the slow ominous beat of the lambegs, the yells of the Catholic residents, Protestants chanting 'Croppies lie down', then a rifle shot followed by screaming.

Conor

Why are you helping me?

Biddy

I don't know why I should. You're a bunch of murderers; criminals with guns who come to our part of town with your sorrowful parade to provoke and kill. And you call yourself protectors, of a country that regards all Irish as dirt, the same way they see former slaves. And you think you have some power. The English Protestant masters want you to blame Catholics for your miseries and see us as threats to what you have; all so you don't blame them, the men of power, the real culprits. I know you have rage but you have the wrong people in your sights. ... Still, if I don't help you I'm no better I suppose.

I saw the director and the casting director glance meaningfully at each other and I knew the audition was a waste of time. I could only imagine what they were communicating and none of it was good. It likely had something to do with my Irish accent. I'd told himself that it was fine but that was when I was rehearsing on my own. Now, working with an Irish actress, I realized that my accent was Oirish in the extreme. All that was missing was an ad lib of 'faith and begorrah'.

I remembered some advice about auditions from an interview with Philip Seymour Hoffman that I'd once read: always do your best and practice your craft in an audition no matter if it becomes a pointless exercise.

> **Cut to**: It is **night**. **Biddy** walks gingerly through the **backyard** of her house. She looks over her shoulder to make sure she's alone and then looks behind the **privy**. She sees nothing. She straightens up in thought and is startled when **Conor** steps out from the shadows.

> **Conor**
> I'm here.

> **Biddy**
> You must go north. Head that way (pointing). Stay out of the street until you get to the next road and then go left.

> **Conor**
> Thank you. My name is Conor. What's yours?

> **Biddy**
> It doesn't matter.

> **Cut to: Conor** starts to leave, then turns to look at **Biddy**. He stares.

> **Cut to: Biddy** who stares back. …

Biddy

Biddy

After the audition, the producer wished me well and said she'd be in touch with my agent.

I signed off my laptop but remained immobile, like a wounded animal taking some time to recover.

I usually felt something like this after a failed audition but this time it was more severe. I'd been awful. I'd reached a new low. Was it time to give up the dream? Maybe I'd been kidding himself about my potential to take on meaty roles.

I continued musing along these lines but eventually rallied. I revived and rescued my dreams with the thought that all I needed was a break and the right part.

My name is Peter Russell. I live in Halifax, Nova Scotia. I'm a server. I work evenings at a downtown restaurant in the Alexander Graham Bell: a boutique hotel.

When I clocked in for my shift that afternoon—sometime shortly after 4:00 PM—I was told that the owner, Charlie Lawrence, would be dining in his suite.

I took the news in my usual way, by nodding assent, and then avoiding the looks of my fellow servers—some of which were bound to be downright hostile stares—and went about the necessary preparations.

My special status was the reason for the nasty looks of my workmates who thought that me being Charlie's sole server was unfair. But it wasn't a role I'd sought, in spite of being told that Charlie tipped exorbitantly.

I was a 'struggling actor' and being Charlie's private server gave me the equivalent of a minimal full-time salary for part-time work—even after half of all my tips, including whatever cash Charlie slipped me, went into the pool to be divided among support staff. It allowed me time to pursue acting roles and to work on getting a fledgling theatre company off the ground.

At 7:30 PM I unlocked Charlie's private elevator on the main floor of the hotel, then wheeled a dinner cart—holding dishes, cutlery, vases, and table linens—into it.

Exiting at the penthouse floor, I crossed the hall and lightly tapped on the door of Charlie's suite. There was no answer, which was as it should be.

Using the key, entrusted to me, I opened the door and pushed my cart inside. I stopped at the first room beyond the entrance foyer: the dining room.

It never failed to impress me with its expensive furnishings, selected by a high-priced decorator no doubt. A showplace meant to manufacture a certain image, a brand, so devoid of any sense of human touch. What it revealed about its owner was absolutely nothing.

I laid out the table, including two vases of flowers.

After that I stood beside the cart, waiting. Eventually, the French doors on the eastern side of the room, swung open.

Charlie's mistress led the way; chin held imperially high, impervious to my presence. She looked to be no more than eighteen or so—considerably less than half Charlie's age certainly. She had blonde hair, like all of Charlie's mistresses (or so I, relatively new to the job, had been told) and she apparently wore the same uniform: short, tight skirt and low cut top with plenty of exposed cleavage.

I'd never heard the woman's name in the six months since becoming Charlie's designated server. And I'd never seen her among the circles of theatre people I hung with so I doubted that she was an aspiring actress.

Charlie, on the other hand, was all smiles when he saw me. All show all of the time. All public relations. "How ya doing Pete?" he said with his cultivated man-of-the-people persona.

I—who never went by Pete—answered that I was fine.

"Good, good."

We were all playing our roles. The down-to-earth boss. the adoring young woman, and me, the discrete waiter.

Soon, Charlie busied himself with a wine list.

I followed my script. "If I can point to the special … Before he left on vacation, Mr. Skelton found a fine bottle of Merlot from Washington State which we're holding for you if you're interested." Mr. Skelton was the restaurant manager.

"Did he now? Merlot, hmm." Charlie made a show of his pedantry, as if weighing his decision, and then pronounced, "Yes, that'll be great." He handed the wine list back to me, with a flourish. Decision made. Turning to his date, he said with a smile, "Nothing but the best. Skelton knows I love Right Bank wine."

The wine special, as always, was something that the manager had picked up especially for Charlie. Something that came in at over $50 a bottle.

At a business lunch, I'd once mistakenly served him a glass of cheap wine of a different type and vintage than the one promised and Charlie had made a great show of swirling, sniffing, and sipping, before pronouncing it wonderful.

Charlie leaned towards his companion and slid his hand under the table in the direction of her thigh. "You're gonna love this wine," he said.

I felt a pang of embarrassment on Charlie's behalf—the self-deluded older man with the woman young enough to be his daughter or granddaughter.

I hoped I'd given him the correct wine and that his dinner companion was of legal drinking age.

I recall a conversation I once had with Lumina on our way to Casey's. I told her that I sometimes wondered what would induce a young woman to have an affair with Charlie.

It wasn't due to loose lips on my part that Lumina knew about Charlie's affairs. She'd figured it out on her own, and since I trusted her discretion I didn't pretend that she was wrong.

I asked, "Do you think there's a quid pro quo there: 'Be nice to me and I'll make you a star'?"

"Could be," said Lumina. "Why?"

"I don't know. Crisis of conscience."

"I've never seen any of the three mistresses he's had—since I've worked at the hotel—in any of his productions. Do you remember what Sharp told us in her class when we were discussing MeToo?"

I remembered Sharp's talk on the matter. She celebrated the fact that women were standing together; demanding to be heard. So, because of that, on top of ending the exploitation of young women, the MeToo movement might shake up the entire industry, and its male dominance. "Which part of what she said?"

"Sharp mentioned something that Susan Sarandon apparently said: that in spite of MeToo there will still be people who have relationships with producers and directors because they're attracted to money and power."

"Are you saying some women might think that being with Charlie is a thrill?"

"God no. Just that, by your own reckoning, we simply don't know what's going on with that woman. She might be getting paid well for the affair for all we know. I've worried about this too: whether I was being complicit in something exploitative. But the fact is that we just don't know."

I had never been able to extract Charlie Lawrence from the social contexts that I saw him in and get a sense of who my employer really was as a person.

Sometimes it was, literally, like studying a specimen under glass. On the nights that Charlie ate at The Seaman's Grill. situated on the hotel's main floor, he'd parade through the restaurant, smiling and shaking hands with the diners, then ensconce himself in his private space—a meeting room that took up the west end of the restaurant, sectioned off behind a glass wall and glass door.

Restaurant patrons often eyed those inside the room, from their seats, and especially when they drifted past on their way to the washrooms.

Inside the room, seemingly oblivious to the attention—but maybe relishing it—Charlie sat at the head of the table, facing the curious.

I gathered that the man had lived in Halifax for about twelve years, and apparently came from Boston.

Charlie referred to himself as a 'Yankee invader' and joked about being the new Governor Lawrence, 'an imperialist here to pillage and conquer'. Since the eighteenth century Nova Scotia governor's actions included the expulsion of Acadians —North America's first instance of ethnic cleansing—and placing a bounty on the scalps of Native men, nobody could accuse Charlie of an excess of compassion.

Stage Direction for the theatrical version of *Playing With Shadows*.

There should be a screen at the back of the stage where we see the shadows of the actors playing in front of it, but which also allows us to see the silhouettes of those performing behind it. The intention of this is to reflect the shadowy nature of many of the characters in the play, but also to conjure up thoughts of Plato's Cave Allegory and the nature of 'reality' after a certain biased education.

> *"In the allegory 'The Cave,' Socrates describes a group of people who have lived chained to the wall of a cave all their lives, facing a blank wall. The people watch shadows projected on the wall from objects passing in front of a fire behind them and give names to these shadows. The shadows are the prisoners' reality, but are not accurate representations of the real world."*
> —Wikipedia

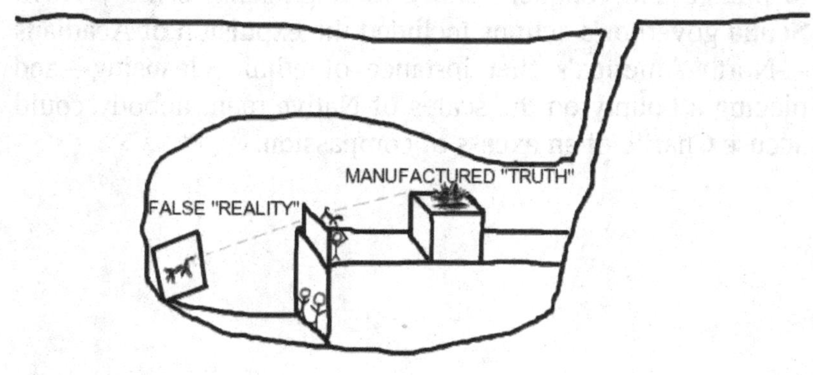

It was Lumina who'd gotten me the job at the hotel.

We were recent graduates of a performing arts program. After graduation, most of our former classmates moved to Toronto, Montreal, Vancouver, and even Los Angeles, but a few of us were determined to try and make a living in the business in Halifax. It had a vibrant theatre scene after all. Plus, it was now common to audition for roles online, so where actors lived wasn't a factor.

Lumina and I had another reason for staying in Halifax: we were developing our own theatre company.

The Other Theatre—consisting of five newly graduated actor-writers—was still in its infancy. Thus far, we'd only done one production, so all five of us maintained gigs on the side to make enough money to survive while the company developed.

Casey's is a noisy place, especially after 11:00 PM.

Lumina and I squeezed between people standing in the crowded aisle as we made our way to a pair of good sized tables in front of a tiny stage at the back of the room where our friends generally clustered.

Besides members of The Other Theatre, the gang at the table was always a variable mix of current theatre and film students, and perhaps a friend or two of one of them. Many of the graduates showed up nightly. The students, as a rule, couldn't afford to do that and were identifiable because four or five of them would be sitting around a pitcher of beer that they'd split the cost of.

My roommate, Ellis, half-stood when she saw me, and waved me to the open seat beside her.

As I sat down I could hear Todd entertaining the group with his latest complaint about his roommate Ronnie. Pretty much everyone there had a roommate but Todd's was generally considered to be the worst. This evening's story involved Ronnie's excessive beer drinking, his frequent peeing through the night with the bathroom door open—loud enough to awaken Todd—and his bragging about how long his pees lasted. It was to the point where he now timed them and bragged about every new record.

While they generally got a laugh, I found the stories more disturbing than humorous.

At times our conversations around Casey's were lively debates about more interesting and controversial topics like how to distinguish someone 'selling out' from being a working actor, coping with ethically challenged directors, on set bullying, and nudity.

I was one of the lucky ones when it came to roommates. Ellis was easy to get along with and a neat freak besides.

Months earlier, after I'd split up with Peggy, and was about to move out of the flat we shared, I discovered that Ellis was also in the market for a new place and roommate. We soon found and leased a second floor apartment in a North End house.

My eyes travelled along the faces of the group around the table. I nodded and smiled at those I made eye contact with. The visual circuit got stuck on Stacey, who smiled back at me.

She was a first year student and new to our table, having been introduced around several weeks before. She was one of the exceptions. Although she was a student, she came into Casey's for a half hour or so every night—like me.

I'd been instantly attracted to her. She impressed me as being smart and interesting. Plus, we were of a similar age—late twenties—and bore the requisite traces of cynicism that came with it.

I don't want to sound neurotic, but I'm certain that she had no immediate interest in me. She never looked my way or responded to anything I said during group conversations.

In spite of that, I found myself watching her and pretending not to. And listening to her while trying to appear to be distracted by something else.

Over the last ten days or so things were different. We still hadn't spoken to each other, one-to-one, but I'd stopped pretending to be indifferent and Stacey, in turn, seemed to focus on me during the group discussions that engaged everyone at the table.

I had this sense that a new story for me was beginning.

Turning to Ellis, I said, "You're up late. What time do you leave?"

"Sh, sh," she whispered.

Drake Cummings, sitting across the table was going on about an ex classmate of ours who would be off in the morning on tour with Charlie Lawrence's latest musical extravaganza. Some groans of derision from people at the table greeted the news.

Ellis didn't want anyone to know that she too was in the production.

Working with Charlie Lawrence—to our friends, intent on doing significant theatre—might well have been the dictionary definition of selling out.

"Six," Ellis whispered in my ear. "My last night of freedom and all that for eighteen days."

"Well break a leg." I tipped the glass of beer that had just arrived in front of me, toasting both Ellis and her boyfriend Gabriel who was sitting on her other side: her partner in selling out.

They tipped their glasses back.

"Was that an invitation to the Charlie Lawrence 'Magnificent Soiree' I saw on the kitchen table?" I asked Ellis. "How'd you swing that?"

"It's Jeff Weird's contribution to my MeToo moment." The theatre director, Jeff Weir, was an older man who'd recently directed a play that Ellis had been in. He was now obsessed with getting her into bed.

"Lovely. It goes without saying, I guess, that you'll be heartbroken about missing the big event."

"Of course. Maybe you should go. Use my invitation."

"Don't you think Jeffie would know I'm not you?"

"You could wear the blonde wig on my dresser. He might never catch on. Borrow any of my clothes you need to make the disguise complete but watch out lest Jeff starts humping your leg."

I smiled at Ellis's joke. I thought it was just a passing bit of sport. I really did. Pretending to be Ellis was a silly idea and not something I would ever contemplate. I mean, who would?

Stage Direction for the theatrical version of *Playing With Shadows*.
To be projected onto the stage screen.

Robin
If we shadows have offended,
Think but this, and all is mended,
That you have but slumbered here
While these visions did appear.
And this weak and idle theme,
No more yielding but a dream …
— William Shakespeare, *A Midsummer
Night's Dream*

Still from 'A Midsummer Night's Dream'

Friday morning.

After breakfast, my agent phoned to say that I wasn't getting the role of Conor that I'd auditioned for the day before.

I was despondent afterwards, despite knowing the news was coming. The call had also served to revive my post-audition self doubts.

It was at my lowest point that I once again noticed Ellis's invitation to the Lawrence soiree, right where she'd left it on the table.

It was the second year for Charlie's mega party. If the stories I'd heard about year one were true, then half of those in attendance would be people from the fields that Charlie worked in: theatre, film, and music. I assumed that this would include filmmakers, theatre directors, and producers.

My understanding was that most of the other invitees would be well-heeled types, like business owners, art dealers, and executives. And having seen a bit of Charlie in action, I imagined that a few politicians would also be on the guest roster. Everyone there to network, to see, and be seen.

The wheels started turning. Why couldn't I do the same? Use my roommate's invitation.

It occurred to me that Ellis was a non-gendered name so I didn't have to show up in drag. If all went well, I could simply walk into the event with her invitation in hand, looking like I belonged. After all, Ellis would be an unknown personage to pretty much everyone there.

I got excited about the idea the longer I entertained it. The soiree might lead to the acting gig that I'd been hoping for. The one that kicked off my career. There were always lots of original and interesting projects going on in the city and getting work in those type of productions would be ideal. Could I afford to miss this chance to meet and impress those working at a local level in film and television?

I headed for my desk, turned on my laptop, and typed into

a search engine: 'tuxedo rentals, Halifax, NS'.

I went to work in the afternoon, as usual.

I was immediately told that Charlie would be dining in his glass-walled room in the restaurant.

All anyone knew about the dinner was that there would be two people in attendance. We never heard the names of those dining with Charlie—not surprising, obviously. It was none of our business.

The dinners were usually business meetings, or so I gathered from the snippets of conversation I overhead when serving him in his private room, and from the few faces I recognized. I'd concluded that Charlie often used the meetings to solicit private and public financial investment for his 'cultural productions'.

Charlie was a self-styled 'cultural entrepreneur'. He'd told me his definition of that on one of the rare evenings when he ate alone.

The aim of the cultural entrepreneur, as Charlie explained it, was to create large scale 'cultural products' (yeah, he really used that term) that generated money and prestige for cities.

To Charlie, that meant that tax dollars should support cultural products—ranging from sports franchises to extravagant musical theatre and massive rock concerts—since these were assets to a city that helped it attract businesses and entrepreneurs to take up residence there.

"We need to respect and enhance our culture, and to 'exploit' (his exact word) local producers. They're our raw product."

Arts workers resented Charlie, not just for the exploitative nature of his work, but because his productions sucked up money that patrons may have otherwise spent supporting local work of various sorts. It was often likened to what happens when a McDonald's or Walmart moves into a town. They kill off local businesses that are unique, variable, and reflective of a specific culture.

Before I arrived on the scene, all of the wait staff used to take turns serving Charlie in The Grill. On the first night that I was given the assignment, just as I was opening the glass door of the private room, I heard Charlie's guest for dinner say, "She's fucking hot. I can hook you up with her no problem."

Charlie glanced alarmingly at me. I looked away and pretended that I'd heard nothing but I obviously had.

After dinner, as Charlie was getting up from the table, he slipped me a hundred dollar bill and said, "I've included a nice tip for everyone to share—as usual. This brown one is just for you, for doing a good job and to let you know that I value loyalty above all."

Well I value loyalty too but I doubted that Charlie and I were thinking of it in the same way. To me, loyalty was a virtue. You aren't coerced into it, and you have nothing to gain by it. You help a friend who needs a job kind of thing. I suspected that Charlie saw loyalty the way a mob boss does (not that Charlie was into anything illegal so far as I knew). Loyalty was the recognition that what was good for you was to shut up. That sort of loyalty wasn't loyalty at all: it was silence through intimidation.

I nodded when handed the hundred and said, "Thank you."

Charlie regarded me for a moment, then smiled, and patted me on the shoulder as if we'd come to an understanding. The next day he told the manager that I was to be his exclusive server on the nights when he ate in the dining room.

A month or so later, I also began serving Charlie's dinners in his suite. Until then, he'd always ordered room service but came down himself to pick up the food trolley in the restaurant.

As always, Friday night found me and Lumina jostling our way up the aisle at Casey's.

Our Monday to Friday evenings almost always concluded with unwinding and socializing at Casey's. Concerts, plays, and films were consigned to the weekend.

Approaching our group of friends, I spotted Stacey. There was an empty chair beside her and that's where I headed.

Stacey had also been coming to the pub on most week nights since her first visit—the one when Leslie introduced her. Leslie had told us that Stacey was enrolled in the same acting program that I'd taken.

After I was settled at the table beside Stacey, and following some mutual smiles and a bit of awkward silence, I found an opportunity to say, "I understand you're an actor. Were you working as an actor before you enrolled at school?"

"A reasonable assumption given that I'm an old lady studying acting, but no, unless you count Leslie's recent student film where I'm 'skinny-dipper number three'."

"I haven't had the pleasure. I'll look out for it."

"And you? Lumina says you actually are an actor. Are you getting some work?"

"Not much, as far as film or TV goes, but since we're including exposing ourselves in student films, my naked butt did appear in Dag Smith's magnum opus about student hi-jinks."

"Brilliant."

"Less memorably, some of us started a small theatre company. We did one production already and are about to start working on our second."

Stacey brightened at that, at the idea, perhaps, of people getting stuff going in the real world.

After answering Stacey's questions about my group, I asked how her courses were going.

"Fine. Strange at times. Something happened today that I haven't been able to stop thinking about."

"What was that?"

"There's a young woman in the same classes as me. We were in the auditorium this morning for a talk by Ronan George …"

"The filmmaker."

"Yes. And there was a Q&A after and this young woman in my program gets up. She says something like, 'I was told by a classmate that a woman needs to be fuckable'—that was her word—'to be a lead actress in films'. And she said that four months ago she saw two lists put together by a group of boys in her high school. One was titled 'Hottest girls' and the other was titled 'Ugliest girls'. She said that her name was on the second list. So she asked Ronan, and she was like, 'Straight up, please be honest. Can I ever get the lead roles I want since they only go to the most sexually attractive women?'"

"Whoa. It takes some serious courage to be so open about something like that."

"I thought so too."

"So what did Ronan say?"

"He was good. He said that reputable filmmakers see actors like any other professional. You hire them based on their skills. His advice to all of us, he said, was to pursue our dreams. So that was fine, but then he started talking about the boys who made the lists and it got interesting."

"How so?"

"Well, he said the list makers weren't talking about beauty —sexual or otherwise—but about their fear of the opposite sex. He said that most teenage boys become interested in females but are terrified of them so they do stuff like make the lists my classmate mentioned to pretend they're in charge. Proof being the list making itself. It strips the girls of their humanity and objectifies them …"

"Like they're a bunch of traits to be shopped for."

"Yes. Ronan said if the boys in this girl's school were like the boys he went to school with, he knew who would be on the lists. The 'hottest' list would be nonthreatening girls. Petite, younger, cute. And the undesirable girls would be the ones who were women: tall, curvy, smart. The boys weren't interested in women. Their mothers were women so, yuck. Women are strong and independent."

"And have libidos ... terrifying."

"Exactly. And then he compared the list maker boys to old school film producers. He said they were the same. These dudes don't make films about older women. Their mothers are older women and they have no personal interest in their stories. They want to work with young women and cast them, even if the male lead is in his fifties. It's not just because they think that young faces sell tickets but because they want to be around women they feel they can dominate."

"So by that token—that these guys are like the high school boys—they're also afraid of women."

"Precisely. That's where I was going. People like Harvey Weinstein are scared of women. Shaking in their boots, like the high school boys. Females are objectified. Sex is about power, and a way to exercise it. They want to deal with young, nonthreatening women."

I laughed. "It's not that I think that's funny but what you said just made me think of something. I could never understand why Weinstein would masturbate in front of women who rejected him. I heard a story of him going into the hotel rooms of women when they slept and masturbating ..."

"That's it. Weinstein had to insist that he was the one in charge and sex was just his method."

"They say that about rapists: that it's about power. ... So if your classmate auditions for some role and the producer turns out to be the old school type she might get a role because she's now the young, non-threatening woman. Hardly seems fair."

"No it doesn't. If she gets roles with these jokers—not for her acting but for her looks—it doesn't mean that all's right with the world for her because she'll soon age out of lead roles."

"Best to avoid men like that."

"Yes, but I'm sympathetic. People have to make a living so it's hard to pick and choose who you work with. And the sexism and paternalism in the performing arts businesses also exists in many other lines of work."

"So what would you have said to her if she'd asked your advice?"

"The same thing I'd say to any eighteen year old. I'd suggest that she pursue her dreams, demand respect, try to work in films and TV with professional environments, and work to reform the industry—if she has a chance. The industry needs women like her so I hope she'll stick with it. … Oh, and I'd tell her not be afraid to tell men to fuck off. Refuse to be silenced. … After all, that's what MeToo is all about isn't it? Women refusing to be silent any longer."

We talked a lot more before closing.

Stacey was a world traveller, I learned, and operated without a net. She would go to a country and find work there, trusting to fate. She'd ended up living and waiting tables in Australia for four years until she was kicked out of the country for being there illegally.

A few months ago she'd returned to Canada with the intention of next setting off for South America, but her parents were excessively worried and offered to pay her way to college or university if she would stay.

And now here she was.

It was well past midnight when everyone at the table began to clear out. Stacey and I kept talking until we were the last two remaining. When the 'last call' horn sounded we agreed that it was time to leave.

We walked out of Casey's side by side, then hesitated on the sidewalk. Stacey said that she was going to the right.

"And me," I said. As we set off together, I added, "You're close enough that you can walk home I gather?"

"Yeah. I live near Barrington."

We were soon involved in a lively discussion about waiting tables. And that segued into talk of favourite filmmakers. Stacey promised to loan me a DVD of Agnès Varda's last film.

We'd begun walking at a rapid pace because of the crisp October air but had slowed considerably by the time we went past my house. I didn't mention that fact. Not from any shyness about the place itself but shyness about appearing too forward. I wanted to invite Stacey in but didn't want to be exposed for the thought.

A short time later she asked, "Where do you live?"

I waved behind us, "A few blocks back. We passed it."

Stacey turned to look but all she would have seen were blocks of old houses, many of which now housed students.

"You should have mentioned it. You could have given me the tour."

I was sorry that I hadn't.

"Did you grow up around here?" Stacey asked.

"No, but my grandfather did. I spent a lot of time in the area when I was a kid so I guess I could claim to be a prodigal son returning. According to Mrs. Tate, my landlady, our street was once an enclave of Irish. It's not anymore and I think Mrs. Tate grieves for it."

We came to a small apartment building and stopped on the sidewalk by the building's front door. "This is me, third floor. … You didn't need to walk me home."

"I enjoyed it."

As we stood and talked some more. I wondered if Stacey was weighing the option of inviting me up. But she abruptly announced that she had plans for first thing the next morning and had to get some sleep.

"I'll see you at Casey's," Stacey said, and quickly disappeared.

Stage Direction for the theatrical version of *Playing With Shadows*.

To be projected onto the stage screen.

Saturday night.

I handed Ellis's invitation to the expensively quaffed matron at the front door who eyed me up and down. Her expression was fierce and judgmental. She was guarding the gates of class privilege after all.

She studied the invitation, apparently assuring herself of its provenance, before putting it with the others piled on her small table. With a sudden engaging smile she said, "Welcome."

I had passed muster. I was now Ellis Downey.

I'd expected chamber music and elegance but the party was a noisy and crowded affair. Soft jazz managed to fight its way out of the background drone. No one was dancing but the night was still young.

The place was awash in free booze but it didn't have a drunken feel to it.

I'd also expected the soiree to be a formal ball, but it wasn't. I was the only person I saw in a tux. Most of the men wore suits, with no ties, while the majority of the women were in dresses. Some had put together especially inventive outfits, makeup, and hair; all demanding attention.

I removed my tie and opened the top button of my shirt.

The entire building and the surrounding grounds had obviously been designed, not for edgy affairs but for fiftieth anniversary and wedding parties between stock portfolios and heirs. Its design mirrored the elements of an ancient Greek temple. I reflected that it was exactly the sort of tastefully designed room that would appeal to Charlie Lawrence.

There were four spots around the room with—what appeared to be—Greek statuary. To my surprise, they turned out to be living people, occasionally changing their poses.

I immediately went to work, squeezing my way around the party on the hunt for networking opportunities.

I spotted Sally Leeson, the independent filmmaker, but she was surrounded by a gaggle of partiers.

I spotted Jeff Weir too, chatting up a young woman. Dressed for success in a natty suit he was all smiles. His supercilious phoniness always made me feel queasy when I was in his presence.

I bagged myself a glass of wine from the tray of a passing server then sized up the crowd. I had no idea how to proceed to network. Perhaps it would be best, I thought, to trust in the ancient Greek gods.

I made my first contact when I ended up squeezed against a woman around my own age who looked familiar. She had platinum blonde hair and wore a glittery and revealing dress that I guessed might have cost as much as the amount I owed in student loans. We smiled at each other and made small talk about the size of the party and the difficulty of navigating around.

"And what to you do?" she asked me.

"I'm an actor."

Drawing her head back to take me in, she said, "Not in one of Charlie's productions?"

"No, I'm part of a small but interesting theatre group."

Well, I hope you enjoy yourself, but I just now see my friend over there. I must run."

The woman squeezed my arm and disappeared into the crowd.

Next up was an older couple. "Oh aren't you handsome," said the lady. "And what is it that you do?"

I told her that I was an actor.

"Oh, how lovely. Have I seen you in anything?"

"Maybe. I'm part of a new theatre company called The Other Theatre. A few months ago we staged our first production; a play about a Syrian refugee family called *The Secret*. It got good reviews ..."

"Well isn't that lovely," the woman said, eyes glazing over.

Her husband, who'd been listening in on the exchange while scanning the room, suddenly tugged at his wife's arm and nodded towards a group of people up ahead.

"Oh, yes, yes," his wife said, coming back to the present. "Well, it was nice to meet you young man." She smiled at me as she walked away, while her husband nodded in my direction.

This interaction—with some variation—was repeated with three other strangers. As soon as I mentioned that I was an unknown actor doing original theatre productions it was zoom and the stranger was gone.

Next up was a man who I was convinced—for some reason—had to be a film producer.

I gave my spiel and the guy wasn't turned off by it, in fact, he appeared to be interested.

I was filled with hope.

"My wife's an actor too," I was told. "That's her over there getting all kissy and huggy with her friends. I hate this whole sort of thing. I'm an academic and would rather be at home with my feet up, a glass of single malt in one hand, and a good book on my lap."

I soon made my excuses and set off in search of other prey, feeling guilty for having quickly become as bloody minded and predatory as the people who'd shunned me.

I soon found myself beside a snack table where I and a young woman began to chat. Our conversation was a refreshing change. I wasn't asked what I did for a living or unduly scrutinized. Instead, we spoke amiably about the food and the party.

The woman was starstruck at the sight of a local CBC celebrity, which I found charming. I liked her: easy to talk to and easy to laugh.

"Just a sec," she said when her cell phone rang. "Where are you?" I overheard her say. As she listened, her face clouded over, as the expression goes. "What? What do you mean things aren't going to work out? You're breaking up with me? Now? Just like that? What kind of coward breaks up with someone over the phone?"

A whole bunch of other weather metaphors occurred to me —involving 'dark skies' and 'storm clouds'—to describe my companion's fierce new demeanour. And then the hurricane blew in.

"You prick!" she shouted loud enough to cause heads to turn, in spite of the generally intense din. Completely without self-consciousness she continued. "Well fuck you too! And watch your back … yeah I am … I know where you live … keep one hand on your balls or they may end up in my …"

I wasn't sure what their possible destination might be because I'd slipped off towards the other side of the room.

I was busy trying to lose myself in the crowd when I came face to face with Charlie Lawrence. The man himself. The host. Shit, I thought.

I'd planned to hide from Charlie since the guy would know I wasn't on his guest list. As well, I'd never mentioned my being an actor to him because I thought he'd likely prefer to be served by someone who wouldn't come into contact with anyone in his social or business circles.

"Pete!" Charlie said with obvious surprise. There was an uncomfortable pause for a split second. Quickly catching himself, Charlie added, "I didn't know you were coming. Ah, you must have come with a friend?"

"Yes."

"Well I'm glad to see you."

He definitely didn't look it, in my estimation.

There was a woman on Charlie's arm. She'd been preoccupied with scanning the party but now turned her head and took me in.

I recognized the platinum blonde hair and glittery dress. It was the first woman I'd spoken to at the party and now I knew why she'd looked familiar. I'd seen her once at the hotel.

"Oh, the actor," the woman said dryly.

"You know each other?" Charlie asked, anxiously looking back and forth.

"We met a little earlier," I said.

"Ah. Pete, this is my wife Addison."

I noticed the emphasis on the word 'wife'; a slight but perceptible communication.

I felt something akin to admiration. Charlie was smooth. The man had perfected the art of maintaining a casual demeanour no matter the circumstances.

I smiled at Addison and it struck me that she had only ever appeared at the hotel restaurant one time during my tenure there, even though Charlie stayed over, in his suite, a few nights every week.

I'd been given to understand that she was an actor but I hadn't seen her on stage. Lumina had though—in a Charlie Lawrence production—and afterwards anointed Addison 'the world's worst actress'. Given the fact that Lumina was a kind-hearted soul, it was a devastating critique.

"Well, I must be moving along," Charlie said. "A lot of meeting and greeting as host, as I'm sure you can imagine. Glad you could make it Pete." He patted my arm.

As he walked away I realized that my heart was pounding.

I was soon reassessing my decision to attend the soiree. Firstly, it was a pointless waste of time—there was no way I was going to network here since everyone was doing the same thing and no one was interested in an out of work actor —and, secondly, I'd maybe just lost my job by being here. And that was without Charlie even knowing that I'd snuck in.

May as well get something out of the visit, I thought.

I detoured back to the food tables where I picked up a dessert plate and scooped up some baking, piling it high, feeling like I'd earned the opportunity to load up on sugar.

Earlier, I'd noted multiple sets of French doors at the south end of the ballroom. They looked to lead out to a patio. I grabbed another glass of wine and headed for the safety of the night outside.

Once through the French doors I spotted a shadowy corner beneath the branches of a huge tree that overhung the stone wall surrounding the patio.

I made a beeline for the spot and discovered that it was indeed, an oasis of solitude: the ideal place to hide and imbibe.

I set my plate and glass down on the wall and looked out. To my left and straight ahead, dissolving into darkness, was a park-like expanse of lawn. On my right was a parking lot. I saw that the fashionably late were still arriving.

I poked my head over the edge of the wall and looked down to see that it was at least four metres to the ground below.

I drew a deep breath of the fresh night air and spread my hands to lean on the wall. It was then that I made the startling discovery that I wasn't alone. My left hand brushed against someone and I immediately recoiled. I hadn't seen the woman because she wore a dark outfit and was standing in shadow.

She was also startled by the contact and moved sideways.

"Oh, sorry," I said, "I didn't see you."

Instead of a verbal reply the shadowy figure slid another foot away.

The frostiness seemed a little much. "Well at least you didn't ask what I did for a living before running away," I said, half under my breath, then went back to studying the parking lot in earnest.

The woman didn't move or say anything, not for awhile,

but eventually she said, "And what is it you do for a living that makes people run away?"

"I'm an obscure actor."

"How awful of you. No wonder."

"I think I'm only meeting people who are here to get something for themselves—to meet beautiful people or to make business contacts—and they don't want to waste their time on a wannabe actor."

"And you didn't come to make contacts?"

"Point taken."

"Well I understand the why but I don't understand the how. How is it that you're here? Nothing personal, but struggling actors aren't the sort who I'd expect to see at a Charlie Lawrence party."

"I used an invitation that was otherwise going to waste."

"I see. Well I don't mean to be antisocial but I'm not here to socialize."

"I always go to parties when I feel like that too."

We lapsed into silence and I used the opportunity to get a better look at my acquaintance and her outfit. She wore a vintage, wide-brimmed hat and trench coat, either black or brown, impossible to say in the dim light. And a large black purse slung over one shoulder, like the one my grandmother used to carry. Was she going for Greta Garbo? Grace Kelly? Maybe a wartime spy.

It struck me that, apart from a quick glance my way, that the woman had remained intensely focused on the people at the party, even when she spoke.

She held a digital camera in one hand. I hadn't noticed it initially but did so when she snapped a photo. She then took another. And after that, she shot a video.

I scooped up my plate of pastries before turning to study the people in her line of vision. "You're paparazzi," I said.

"Indeed."

But what was there to see, I wondered? Not a movie star in sight. And why was this woman operating from a dark corner like she wished to avoid detection? There were several photographers circulating. Apparently media exposure was desirable and none of the guests appeared to be objecting.

I shrugged. My sweets awaited and I went back to them.

"This is very nice basma," I said, as much to myself as to the woman in the shadows.

Her head turned to look. "Isn't it baklava?"

"Of a sort. It's a Lebanese variety."

"Are you Lebanese?"

"No, I live near a Lebanese coffee shop."

"Oh, I don't know the place. I'm not from Halifax."

"Your accent, if I may ask, New Zealand?"

"Very good, yes."

"And what's the quintessential New Zealand pastry?"

"I don't know. I like Anzac biscuits—a kind of coconut cookie."

"So not mince on toast?"

"Not precisely a pastry. How do you know about Kiwi food?"

"There's an Australian and New Zealand restaurant on Robie that I've been to. A cafe actually."

"I know the place. I live in a flat nearby."

I observed two men in cheap suits come through the French doors. Their attire screamed 'party security'.

They stopped just beyond the doors and craned their necks, looking back and forth, taking in the dozens of people on the expansive patio.

The woman's reaction was visceral. I felt it more than saw it. She spun so that her back was to the men.

As they began to circulate among the guests—their heads bobbing here and there, peering into people's faces to examine them—I watched the woman slip her camera into her purse.

She rapidly sidled off to her left, keeping her head down and her back to the party.

She edged her way to the end of the patio where there was an opening in the stone wall. She slipped through it.

I shifted my attention back to the cheap suit guys but didn't immediately spot either.

I recoiled, startled, when one of them suddenly appeared directly in front of me. He shoved his face up close to mine and studied me.

I felt vulnerable—the guy gave me the creeps plus I was here under false pretenses. I managed to placidly look back at him, chewing my basma like a cow working its cud.

The cheap suit guy moved on.

Just then, I noticed a third man—this one was expensively dressed—come through the French doors and begin looking about.

The security guy who'd lately been in my face must have seen him too because he pushed his way through the crowd to join the nice suit guy; his boss presumably.

While the two were standing face to face the boss spoke animatedly, jabbing his finger in the direction of the patio exit.

When the other security guy joined them the pantomime was repeated.

Both of the security guys then set off across the patio. They exited via the same portico the mysterious photographer had taken.

The man in the expensive suit, meanwhile, returned to the ballroom.

Why was security following the woman, I wondered? Was she a jewel thief? I laughed at the thought. If she'd stolen something she wouldn't have been standing around watching the party and snapping photos. I'd watched too many old movies. In my defence though, the mystery woman's costume was straight out of a Hitchcock film.

Was the fact that she'd been taking photos and video the issue? If the security company's job included chasing away unaccredited paparazzi, I would have understood if they'd scolded her and asked her to leave, but she'd already gone when the two security men had set out after her. Surely it wasn't to say 'hi' and wish her well.

I set down my plate on the wall and went in search of the woman from the shadows.

I passed through the portico and stepped onto a patch of lawn. A relatively quiet space measuring about 10x10 metres. It was surrounded by a line of trees straight ahead and by boxwood hedges to the left and right.

All three borders had gaps in the middle of them with walkways visible beyond.

Because of the scant light cast by two faux streetlamp fixtures, I could discern the shapes of four couples; standing, chatting, and smoking one thing or another.

There was no shadow woman to be seen. Not a single guy in a cheap suit either.

The path beyond the gap in the wall of trees ahead, looked to run to the right, into what was likely a forested area. Going through the hedges on either side of me would lead to wide open park.

Since the forest would be the obvious choice to hide, if I was a fifties era spy in a tench coat, I crossed the lawn.

I soon found myself on a wide path, with rocks bordering both sides. I began to walk along it, through the forest.

The path was devoid of artificial lighting so it grew increasingly difficult to see the further I moved away from the smoker's lawn. There was just enough moonlight for me to navigate if I stayed halfway between the silhouetted walls of bush on each side.

It also grew quieter and quieter the further I got from the party.

Hearing a voice ahead, I stopped.

It was a male voice; loud and aggressive.

Creeping forward, I managed to make out the shape of a man's back, two metres away. It was one of the security guys. He appeared to be holding the shadow woman. Each of his hands clutched one of her arms, pinning them to her sides.

I edged sideways, towards the cover of the bush, when my foot bumped against the rock border.

Security guy #2, the owner of the loud voice, was striding

back and forth in front of his partner and the shadow woman. He was ranting, "You were told and told to stay away Vanessa, and to go home. Why didn't you listen? And now we have no choice about what's going to happen, do we?"

I reached down. Got my hand around a good sized boulder.

Security guy #2 stepped forward. He punched Vanessa in the stomach. She gave a little yelp and bent over.

The man grabbed her hair. Forced her head upright. Raised his fist to punch her in the face.

I stepped up behind security guy #1 and slammed him on the back of the head with my boulder. He slumped to his knees and let go his grip on Vanessa.

Security guy #2 froze. Still clutching Vanessa's hair. A fist still raised. He stared straight ahead, clearly confused. The spot where his fellow goon had been was now just my chest.

My arm arced over Vanessa as I pounded #2 between the eyes with my rock.

He fell backwards. And released his grip on Vanessa.

There were now two guys in cheap suits curled up on the path. Moaning, groaning, and cursing.

I took Vanessa's arm. "Run!" I said in her ear.

She straightened up. Looked intently at me. Then bolted off. But back towards the party!

I watched her go. There was no way I was going in that direction.

I noticed something on the ground: Vanessa's purse. I scooped it up. I saw Vanessa's hat. Grabbed that too.

And I ran off into the void.

After sprinting for maybe fifty yards, I stopped.

Why was I running? I looked behind me and listened. Nothing.

I walked to my right. Stumbled over the rock border.

I tentatively moved towards the shape of a giant maple tree standing no more than a metre from the path. And I slipped behind it.

Out of sight from any pursuers, I leaned against the tree and caught my breath. I watched and listened. No sounds of pursuing goons.

Would they come after me? I hoped not. There were two of them and I wouldn't have the advantage of surprise if they caught me. And I had dropped my bloodied boulder.

I quickly dismissed the possibility of pursuit. It seemed more likely that the goons would head back to the party. Vanessa was their target and she'd gone in that direction. And if they hadn't watched her go—being a little distracted—they would likely function on automatic and head back to base.

I tried to locate myself. When I was standing on the patio with Vanessa I'd been facing an expanse of lawn running southwards. There were trees on my left and the parking lot on my right.

Setting off after Vanessa, I'd gone in the direction of the trees. At the forest path, I turned right, which meant I'd been travelling parallel to the lawn. Which also meant that the parkland was on the other side of the strip of trees where I was now standing.

I blindly edged my way forward. The darkness was so dense beneath the tree canopy that all I could do was gingerly swing my arms out in front of me, back and forth like antennae, feeling my way along and testing every step before making it.

Ten minutes later, I stepped out of the bush and onto lawn. I looked to my right. Perhaps the length of a football field away was the smoker's lawn.

I set off, creeping along the edge of the trees, staying in their shadows.

I could make out the sound of the jazz band, and the muted laughter and buzz of partiers, but I heard no voices. Not even when I got to the area that I reckoned would be directly beside the spot where—on the other side of the trees—the goons had attacked Vanessa. Not a moan or groan to be heard.

I steeled himself when I got to the hedge that edged the smokers' lawn.

I opened Vanessa's purse and put her hat inside, trying not to crush it. Luckily the bag was enormous and there wasn't much inside. Taking off my jacket, I wrapped the purse in it. Tucked it under my arm. Took a deep, actor's breath.

I passed through the break in the hedge, and onto the lawn. The area had begun to fill up with people smoking dope, judging by the smell.

I crossed the lawn and went through the portico in the rock wall, back onto the patio where my circuit had begun.

It wasn't until I was making my way through the French doors of the ballroom that it occurred to me that neither of the goons had seen my face in the light.

I breathed easier after that. Walked a little taller. Struck a bold attitude to say that I belonged.

The music was now cranked. And the lights were dimmed. Folks were dancing, and the room had that drunken feel to it: that fertile environment for sentimentalism, hedonism, false wisdom, and aggression.

I circulated around the ballroom, dodging bodies and searching every face. No Vanessa.

With nothing more to do that I could think of, I made my way out of the building through the front entrance, past the gate keeper protecting classism and celebrity, and into the parking lot.

I headed up the paved drive that led through the park-like acreage and began my long walk home.

Stage Direction for the theatrical version of *Playing With Shadows*.
To be projected onto the stage screen.

Jazz music should play throughout the entire soiree episode with the volume escalating at this point. Same thing with a tape loop of people's voices, talking, laughing, etc. Consider using a stage smoke/fog machine when we see these people, outside the party, by the patio wall.

What I didn't know, and didn't find out until much later, was that Vanessa, after running from the security goons, had gone all the way back to the smoking area before the fact that she didn't have her purse impressed itself upon her. Its contents were indispensable.

She considered the problem before making the potentially deadly decision to retrace her steps back to where she'd been attacked.

She silently crept along the trail. Hearing approaching voices, she stepped into the bush and knelt behind a shrub.

As the two goons dragged themselves past her, Vanessa heard them commiserating and swearing in a semi-articulate manner about the holy terrors they'd unleash on her the next time they saw her and the special treatment they'd mete out to the man who coshed them with the rock.

Vanessa waited a suitable length of time before emerging from the bush and walking to the area where the assault had occurred.

After seeing nothing in the darkness, she got down on her hands and knees and patted the ground over a two metre radius. Still nothing.

Exasperated, she eventually followed the path back towards the party.

Instead of going back to the patio when she reached the outside smoking lawn, Vanessa turned south and went through the boxwood hedge's opening. She turned to her right and walked along the base of the high rock wall of the patio, back to the parking lot. From there she followed the driveway to the street where she hailed a cab to Dartmouth.

What Vanessa didn't know, and didn't find out until much later, was that a man in a posh suit, standing in the same shadows on the patio where she'd earlier stood while spying on the party goers, had spotted her passing below and was now following her in a second cab.

The house was asleep when I got home. The ever vigilant Mrs. Tate, on the first floor, had retired for the night.

In order not to waken her, I crept softly up the stairs and into my darkened apartment.

I immediately went to bed but given all that had happened at the soiree I couldn't calm myself enough to sleep. The bewildering events of the evening played round and round in my thoughts, demanding answers—but none came.

I got up several times to roam the apartment in the dark, creaking my way over the floorboards of the ancient house, cursing each crunch, imagining old Mrs. Tate waking up with every one of them. She had the hearing of a bat—an 'old bat' in my estimation—and I had no doubt that she would vociferously complain to me about my pacing the next time we met on the stairs.

I found himself going to the front window, over and over, to survey the street below as if there might be something to see there.

Resigning myself to the fact that sleeping was impossible, I eventually sank into the easy chair in the livingroom where I remained absorbed with my questions. The principal ones were: Who was Vanessa and why had the security goons attacked her?

I knew nothing about the unusually dressed woman so I didn't make any advance there. She was a shadowy personage in every sense. I didn't know if I'd even recognize her if I saw her again.

As to the actions of the security goons, I struggled to come up with any reason why someone taking some paparazzi photos would be physically attacked.

And what sort of photos or videos would Vanessa have gotten from standing in a dark corner and capturing people from a distance? Other than poorly lit photos, nothing came to mind.

I had overheard goon #2 say to Vanessa that she'd been

warned off earlier, so they obviously had a history, either at the party or somewhere else. What could have been so important to her that Vanessa would have continued to take photos despite the risk of physical harm to herself?

There was no way of knowing the answer to that so I took a different tact. Who was being protected by the goons? The obvious answer was Charlie Lawrence. It was his party so he was presumably the one who'd engaged this particular security company.

What did it say about Charlie that he'd employ a company that beat people up? It was the kind of thing you'd expect from organized crime. Still, I thought, I needed to reserve judgment until I was in possession of more facts. I was no fan of Charlie Lawrence but I'd never heard anyone suggest that he was involved in criminal pursuits.

Maybe the goons were protecting someone other than Charlie, I thought. The soiree had been filled with wealthy and influential people. Was Vanessa a detective spying on a person who wanted to be discrete? Maybe the circulating photographers had been told not to photograph that person and the security goons were enforcing the rule.

Sunday.

I don't recall when it happened but I'd eventually dozed off in the easy chair in the livingroom.

It was 9:15 AM when I woke up with a sore back.

I struggled to my feet. Standing up straight, I clasped my hands behind my back. After several stretches I bent forward and touched my toes a few times. I next put my hands on my hips and began to make circles with my head. It was on my second or third rotation when I spotted Vanessa's purse sitting on the coffee table. I stopped in mid arc and stared at the bag. What was I to do with the thing? How was I going to get it back to Vanessa?

Turning it over to the Lost and Found at the party—if there was one—wasn't an option since it would give the security people Vanessa's camera. I didn't know what was on it but I was on her side and certainly not on that of goons who beat people up.

I'd opened the purse to put Vanessa's hat inside and saw that the camera wasn't the only thing in there. Maybe there was a cell phone or something with an address on it, I thought.

I began to reach into the bag, but hesitated. The idea of searching it felt like an invasion of privacy. Considering the matter, I decided that rifling through the purse would be my final option.

When I was putting some jam on my toast it brought to mind the Australian and New Zealand cafe that served mince toast. Vanessa had said that she lived near it.

A plan of action began to percolate with the coffee. After breakfast I would head to the cafe. Maybe they knew Vanessa and could give me her address. Maybe they'd be willing to hold the bag until they saw her.

As a last resort, if going to the cafe didn't solve my

dilemma, I could walk around the neighbourhood and, with any kind of luck, I might spot Vanessa.

Walking aimlessly around a part of town, trusting in serendipity, wasn't much of a back-up plan so far as back-up plans went—especially since I couldn't even picture Vanessa's face—but it was the only one I came up with.

Perhaps, I told himself, something else would occur to me once I was in the Dartmouth neighbourhood.

And so it was that, later that Sunday morning, I got off the bus near Robie and Duffus with Vanessa's purse in my backpack, slung loosely over my shoulder.

The Golden Wattle & Silver Fern turned out to be closed for the day, being Sunday.

I chastised myself for not having considered the possibility, but decided to proceed with Plan B since I was already in the neighbourhood.

Beginning at the cafe, I systematically walked up one street then down the next for several blocks in each direction.

There was no sign of my quarry. No sign of just about anyone in fact. Exactly what you'd expect on a sleepy Sunday morning.

After concluding my route, I set out to cover it again. Back and forth, street after street. Same result. Vanessa was an elusive target.

And then I followed the route yet again. The community had gradually awakened during my walks and I was seeing more and more residents out and about with each tour. People working in their gardens. Sitting on their front steps.

When I passed them for the first time they had generally said 'hello' but I was now at a point where I was walking past some of them for the third time that morning—and always travelling in the same direction. Self-conscious, I avoided returning anyone's gaze.

At one point I realized that I was being followed by a burly man who looked like he may have designated himself as neighbourhood watch. The guy trailed me for three blocks before disappearing.

It wouldn't have surprised me if a police cruiser had pulled up beside me.

It was a working class area and almost all of the houses were small, single story bungalows. Vanessa had said that she lived in a flat so I decided to knock on the front door of every two-storey place I came to. She must live in one of them.

At the first such house, a little macho dog in protective mode set up an insane barking. A voice could be heard ordering the dog to 'shut it down' before a middle-aged man swung open the front door. He looked to be annoyed, like I was someone looking to convince him that I knew the way to save his soul. He asked, "What can I do for you?"

"I'm looking for a woman name Vanessa," I said. "She was at a party last night and left her bag behind. She told me she lived around here, by The Golden Wattle & Silver Fern Cafe. She has a New Zealand accent. Yay high." I held up a hand. "Dark hair."

"No," said the man, shaking his head. "Let me ask my wife." He disappeared into the house.

I heard him talking softly in the background before a woman of the same vintage appeared at the door. "You're looking for a woman who works at the restaurant on Robie?"

"The Golden ... No, not someone who works there. A woman left her purse at a party I was at. She told me she lives near the restaurant."

"Is there ID in the bag?"

"I didn't look."

The woman stared at me like I was dense. "Do you want me to look?"

"No."

"Well, if you want my opinion, you should return the purse to wherever the party was and leave it there. That's where the lady will look for it, I think. Maybe the people who own the house will know how to contact her."

"The party wasn't at a house and I don't think they have a Lost and Found."

Suddenly, obviously wary of me, the woman said, "Then you should go to the police. We can't help you, Sorry." She abruptly closed the door in my face.

I didn't blame her for being suspicious. If someone came to my door with a story like mine I'd have suspected them of being a stalker too.

I gave up on the idea of knocking on random doors. My quest was futile. A waste of time.

I headed for a nearby fast food joint to use their washroom and get myself a coffee. After that, I settled at a table by the front window and watched the traffic pass.

I noticed a bus pull up to a stop directly in front of the restaurant and disperse some passengers. It spawned an idea. Work and school draw people out of their houses. If I were to return the next day, on Monday, and I came early, I could keep my eye on the bus stops on each side of the street as people headed out. Vanessa might show up at one of them. She hadn't said what she did for a living but she must have a job since, if she was a tourist, she'd be staying at a hostel or a hotel.

If I didn't spot her, I thought, I could hang around until the cafe opened and speak to the people who worked there.

I was about to head home when I decided that I'd had enough. I'd done my best to respect Vanessa's privacy and not root through her purse, but it was time to think of myself. I opened the purse.

After removing Vanessa's hat, I pulled out the camera I'd seen in use the night before at the soiree and put it aside.

In the bag was an envelope addressed to one Vanessa Sutherland at an address in Halifax.

I pitched my coffee in the garbage without having taken a sip and left the restaurant.

I knew Vanessa's street well enough. I'd been up and down it three times without seeing her.

The house I headed for was indeed close to the New Zealand restaurant, a two-storey place no more than a one minute's walk away. If I'd continued knocking on doors it would have been next up.

I saw two mailboxes on the wall beside the front door of the house. The tag on one box said 'Page' and the tag on the other said, 'Steele'.

I tapped on the door.

The curtain behind the door's window was soon pulled

back and the face of a small, grey-haired woman popped up then immediately disappeared.

The door opened a few inches and her face appeared in the opening. "Yes?"

"I'm looking for Vanessa Sutherland. Is she here?"

"No. I already told your people, not five minutes ago, that she's not here. I heard her leave this morning and she hasn't come home."

"My people?"

"Yes, Immigration. When I see her again I'm asking her to pack up her stuff and leave. I don't want her here. I live quiet and I don't need any trouble. She's a nice girl but I didn't know she was in the country illegally."

"She's here illegally?"

"Don't you know? Your men told me she was."

"I'm not from Immigration."

"Who are you then?" The woman recoiled, obviously leery.

"I'm just … I'm Vanessa's friend."

"Well I don't know where she is, sorry." And with that the woman closed the door.

In 24 hours, being rejected had become my new normal.

As I walked towards Robie I passed an SUV parked a couple of doors away from Vanessa's house. As I went by I happened to glance inside. And there they were, watching: the two goons!

I was close to home. My heart had almost stopped when I spotted the goons in Dartmouth but I'd had plenty of time to calm down since then—and to consider the matter. Not least of the things under consideration was the question of why they hadn't jumped me. The obvious answer was that they didn't recognized me because they hadn't gotten a good look at me the previous night.

After walking past the Lebanese coffee shop which sold the basma I'd told Vanessa about, I turned east onto the street where I lived.

I hadn't gone more than four or five metres when I heard footsteps behind me.

"You're a hard person to find."

I glanced to my right to see who'd fallen into step beside me. It was a woman with a trench coat slung over one arm. "Vanessa! I'm glad you're okay. I wondered if I'd ever see you again."

"You know my name."

"Yeah, I heard one of your friends use it last night."

"Oh, of course. Those two are a lot of things, but friends isn't one of them. It doesn't matter. I've been hanging around the Lebanese bakery, all day, hoping to find you to say thanks for your help. I don't know what I would have done without you. And now here you are. So thank you."

I laughed at the irony. While I'd been searching Vanessa's neighbourhood she'd been searching mine.

Vanessa continued walking beside me for a few more steps before squeezing my arm and saying, "I'll leave you to your Sunday."

As she began to turn, I said, "Just a sec. I have something of yours."

We both stopped and I scrambled to pull the backpack off my shoulder. I removed her purse from the backpack and held it out.

"My bag! You have it!" Reaching for it, she added, "I

thought my non-friends took it. I never thought I'd see it again."

"I was beginning to think the same thing. I spent my day walking the neighbourhood around the cafe you mentioned yesterday. You're a hard person to find."

Vanessa was only momentarily puzzled. "The cafe? ... Oh, the Kiwi place. Thank you for that."

"I'm sorry but I finally broke down and opened the purse to get your address."

"My address was in my bag?"

"There's an envelope with your address on it." I reached towards the purse but stopped myself.

"An envelope?" Her perplexed expression cleared almost immediately. "Oh right, the letter from my sister. It was in my mailbox when I left home yesterday so I stuck it in my bag to read later."

"When I found you weren't home, I decided to give your purse to the lady who also lives in your building but she more or less slammed the door in my face."

"Mrs. Page slammed the door in your face?" Vanessa was incredulous.

"Yeah. She was upset. She said that some men from Immigration showed up looking for you because you're here illegally. She said that when you came home she was going to ask you to move out because she didn't want any trouble."

"Immigration? They couldn't have been. I'm not here illegally."

"I know. As I was walking away from your place I passed an SUV. The two security goons from last night were sitting in it, watching. My guess is that they were the so-called Immigration men."

"What! How do they know where I live?" ... Vanessa went silent, considering the matter. She slowly said, "But there was no one outside when *I* left home."

"Your landlady said they'd just been to her door, so they probably only came later."

"If it was the guys from last night, why didn't they attack you for conking them on the head?"

"I doubt they saw my face."

"I better go see Mrs. Page and explain. I guess they're trying to get me booted from my place so I'll leave the country."

"Or, that could have just been a story to get your landlady to let them into the house. I've been thinking about it, and about what happened to you last night, and I wonder if that's why they went to your apartment—to finish what they started."

Vanessa seemed to consider the matter before saying, "I guess you're right. Damn."

She looked at me and shrugged, defeated, then resumed walking, once again going in my direction, having seemingly come to the conclusion that she had nowhere in particular to go.

I fell into step beside her but remained silent. "That's me," I soon said, pointing at a two-story house just ahead. "Why don't you come up and consider your options."

Vanessa said 'okay' in an automatic way, and I wasn't sure if she'd even heard what I'd said.

"Just a heads-up," I said, trying to lighten the mood, "if an old lady comes flying out the door of her apartment and tries to wheedle it out of me who you are, don't worry. It's my landlady—who's also the owner. She's excessively officious and nosy."

We turned up the walkway leading to my front door and I saw that, as luck would have it, Mrs. Tate wasn't at her command post at the front window of her main floor apartment.

Vanessa and I were already up the stairs and inside my flat when Mrs. Tate's apartment door could be heard opening. Likely planning to discuss my pacing the previous night.

I whispered something under my breath along the lines of, "Better buy some trainers you old busy body."

"Do you want coffee?" I asked Vanessa when she arrived back in the kitchen from the bathroom. "Or maybe a cup of tea?"

"I don't want to put you out, but tea would be nice."

I put the kettle on. "Please, have a seat," I said, pointing to a kitchen chair. "Do you want to charge your phone?" I hadn't seen one in her bag so assumed I'd just missed it.

"Thanks, but I don't have a phone."

I absorbed the answer with a passing thought that not having a phone was unusual.

After the kettle boiled I poured some hot water into a teapot, put it on the table, and sat down opposite Vanessa. It was the first time I'd gotten a clear look at her. She had black, shoulder length hair and intelligent eyes with more wrinkles around them than usual for her age, which I estimated to be mid-thirties.

"Do you have somewhere to go?" I asked.

"Yeah, back to my flat."

"I mean apart from going home."

"... Then I guess I have nowhere to go."

"So no friends whose place you could stay at?"

"No. I've only been in the country a few weeks and I work from my apartment."

"Can I ask you who those guys that attacked you are and why they did that?"

"You can ask and I know it's maybe not fair not to tell you but I'd rather not. ... Sorry."

"That's okay. It's not like it's any of my business."

"Do you know of a motel in the area that's dirt cheap? Oh, and that isn't too scuzzy."

"Ah ... I don't ... How long would you be staying?"

"A couple of weeks, then I head for New Zealand."

"I thought you lived here."

"No. My apartment is an Airbnb that I rented for six weeks."

"Ah, since the name Sutherland wasn't on either of the mailboxes I assumed that you lived there with someone else."

"No, just me."

"I can point you in the direction of some motels but I don't know anything about them. They don't scream glamour, so I assume they're not too expensive but that's just a guess."

"Thanks."

As I was pouring our tea, I impulsively said, "I hope this doesn't sound weird but, my roommate's away for a few … let me see … for a little over two weeks. She's the one whose ticket I used to get into the soiree … that's her room at the end of the hall. You can crash here, in her room I mean, if you want to. You'd be welcome."

Vanessa looked intently in my direction. "Why would you help me?"

"It seems you need it."

"Your flatmate's an actor too?"

"And then some. She sings and dances, and is currently in Charlie Lawrence's huge musical production."

Vanessa's antenna went up at the mention of Charlie's name. There was no mistaking it.

I continued, "Check out the room. Ellis is cool. She won't mind. It's not a big place, I know, but it's comfortable enough."

Before the house had been divided into two apartments, the upper floor had been four bedrooms and a bathroom. One of the bedrooms now served as a livingroom and another had been converted into a kitchen. The renovators had left the two tiniest rooms as bedrooms.

Vanessa went to look at Ellis's room. She was gone a full minute—assessing more than the room I assumed.

I was also doing some thinking, wondering if I'd acted too quickly in inviting a woman that I didn't know to move into my apartment. A woman who was mixed up in some possibly dangerous business. And it wasn't even my room that I was offering her.

It occurred to me that I should get permission from Ellis before loaning out her room but I'd already made the offer of it to Vanessa. It wouldn't be fair to qualify it now.

On returning to the kitchen, Vanessa said, "I don't want to put you out."

"You wouldn't be. I'm almost never here."

"I'd want to give you some money for the room and of course I'll buy my own food."

"No money for the room. It's paid for. I'm not looking to profit from your misfortune. Buying your own food, yeah that's fine … but starting tomorrow."

"Then I accept. Thank you."

I spent what was left of the afternoon on my laptop, in my room, while Vanessa lay down in hers.

For dinner, I made spaghetti.

We'd been eating for several minutes when I broke the silence. "The apartment and house keys are on hooks by the door. I'll warn you though, our landlady spends her time scrutinizing the neighbourhood and us, her tenants. She may pounce on you going up or down the stairs and ask you who you are. Even though she's old, she's stealthy, and fast like a Ninja. If you want to escape her you've got to race down the stairs as soon as you open the apartment door."

"I look forward to meeting her."

The budding conversation soon fell off.

Eventually Vanessa asked if I was acting in a play.

I set down my fork, happy to give all my attention to my current passion: The Other Theatre. "Not at the moment but some friends and I began a theatre company after graduation with the idea that we would do original, politically oriented works. We did one play: a portrait of a Syrian refugee family. Tomorrow afternoon we're having a meeting to plan our second production, so hopefully we'll soon be working on something else."

"Do you ever get any other roles?"

"I've done a couple of small things."

"So it makes sense to have your own theatre group to get your name out there … and I guess it's a creative outlet too."

"Exactly. We're actors. We'll whither up and die without an audience and attention."

"Did you ever work with Charlie Lawrence's wife? I understand she's an actor."

The question reminded me that I still knew nothing of Vanessa and why she'd been at Charlie's soiree. The fact that she knew his wife was an actor indicated that she knew something about him.

"No … I mean, yes, she's an actor but no, I've never

worked with her. It's maybe just as well. Lumina—one of my co-workers at the restaurant and also a member of my theatre group—calls Addison 'the world's worst actor'."

"And is that a fair assessment?"

"I haven't seen Addison act in anything to judge but Lumina is always supportive of other women so if she says a woman can't act I assume it's true."

"If you don't mind my asking; can you get by financially on your acting work or do you have another job?"

"I'm the embodiment of the cliché about actors. I work part-time as a server in a restaurant."

"Which one?"

"It's called The Seaman's Grill. It's the restaurant in Charlie Lawrence's boutique hotel."

"You work for Charlie!" Vanessa froze, a forkful of spaghetti halfway to her mouth. "I didn't realize you were his friend. I guess that explains why you were at his party." There was a palpable chill in Vanessa's tone of voice which until then had been light and friendly. It was the second time that she'd reacted this way to the mention of Charlie's name. She clearly didn't like him.

"Well, no. I snuck in to tell you the truth. Or rather I used Ellis's invitation which was going to waste. I thought I might be able to make some contacts. Speaking of waste, the whole thing was a waste of time."

Vanessa set down her fork and reached for her glass of water. She took a sip and carefully said, like she wanted to be absolutely certain of the facts, "So, you're not friends?"

"I'm just a lowly server in his restaurant. I certainly don't reach the threshold of wealth or power to make myself friend material to someone like Charlie Lawrence."

Still speaking slowly and deliberately, Vanessa said, "Your roommate had an invite to the party. Is she Charlie's friend?"

"No. One of Charlie's pals is a theatre director named Jeff Weir and he's got a thing for Ellis. An unhealthy thing, but anyway, he apparently swung the invite."

"So what's your opinion of your boss?"

"I don't know him, I mean, not personally. He's always very nice, and friendly with me, but he's an expert in PR so I put it down to that. It's hard to see beyond his surface facade. … I guess my attitude is a bit cynical. As an actor—someone working in theatre—I'm very critical of what he does. He stages these extravagant productions that he calls 'cultural commodities'. I have no interest in them because I don't think that vibrant theatre is local versions of film musicals and the like. … I mean, everybody's free to do what they want but his productions harm people doing original and significant work. His stuff overshadows their plays, sucking up money and audiences."

"But you still work for him."

"I just work for him in his hotel—not in any capacity related to his spectacles. I'm his exclusive food server when he's there so I get very good tips. I have no love of the job but the gratuities give me enough to pay the bills and let me focus on my real career. That's not a thing that a struggling actor can lightly pass up."

"A private server. How did you land that gig?"

I detected a hint of suspicion in the way the question was asked, like I'd maybe done something nefarious to get my special status at work.

"I was Charlie's server one night and I overheard something. Later, after the meal, he slipped me a huge tip, and he made it clear that the money was to keep what I'd heard to myself. I took the money and after that, Charlie told the manager that I'd be his exclusive server if I was working that night."

"So he pays you to be discrete." Before I had a chance to respond, Vanessa added, "Can I ask what you overheard?"

"It was a sexist sexual comment by his crony about hooking Charlie up with some woman … I suppose he's worried about his image. He considers his extravaganzas to be family fare." I broke off and took a sip of tea. I was drifting into the personal Charlie and wanted to stop things moving in that direction.

"You must hear some juicy tidbits," Vanessa prompted.

"I'm not into listening to intimate stuff."

"No, I don't mean personal stuff—yes, that would be pretty gross in Charlie's case. I meant hearing inside dope on his business dealings and … I'm sure he's into all sorts of odd things."

"I never overhear anything of that nature. Charlie has a loud voice and I might catch words here and there but they have no context so it's meaningless. He entertains his dinner guests in his private dining room that's within the restaurant. Its walls are glass so he and his guests can see me coming and I get the impression that everyone shuts up when I'm about to enter. … So, do you think Charlie's involved in some dicey business affairs?"

"I don't know anything about the man."

I got up from the table and put my empty plate in the sink. Vanessa was still eating. The interlude allowed me a moment to think. Her last statement felt like a lie, to put it bluntly. It seemed obvious to me that she did know some things about Charlie, and given her attitude when she spoke about him, her impression of him was highly negative. It further suggested that the attack on her was connected to Charlie.

Surprisingly, I didn't feel any resentment about having to explain myself. Whatever was going on, I wasn't on the side of the aggressor, which in this case was Charlie, so I was happy to assure Vanessa that I wasn't connected to him.

Sitting back down at the table, I said, "I've never heard of Charlie doing anything illegal. But then again, why would I? I never speak to anyone who's on close terms with him. Ellis said that the production she's in is being done on the cheap, and she's pretty put off by the way it was rushed to the stage, but I haven't heard that Charlie's ripping anyone off or anything like that."

"No, of course. And maybe his dinner guests aren't business people but friends."

"I think it's a bit of both but that's just a guess."

Something struck me. If Vanessa had to guard against possible physical attacks maybe I did too while she was staying at my place. Being kept in the dark meant that I didn't know who I had to stay on guard against. Or why.

It didn't feel fair that Vanessa would tell me nothing but I bit my lip and remained quiet about the matter.

Monday.

In the morning Vanessa and I ate breakfast together.

She looked exhausted, in spite of the fact that she'd gone to bed almost immediately after dinner the previous evening.

It wasn't surprising. I'd heard her get up and move about in her room several times in the night. She was obviously in an extremely stressful situation.

Vanessa didn't seem to be in a mood to talk so I stayed silent for the most part.

Abruptly Vanessa said, "I was thinking about it and I feel that I owe you an explanation about the other night."

"I don't think …"

"No, I do. Of course you'll want to know if you're harbouring a criminal under your roof or if the men who attacked me are going to swoop down on you too. … So, where to start? I came to this country looking for my six year old daughter. Her father, whom I'm separated from, took her and brought her to Canada."

"You mean, he took her from New Zealand?"

"Yes. Ev—the father—never had any particular interest in Sam—my daughter. That is, until two months ago, when he picked her up one day, supposedly for a couple of hours—which was the extent of his visits—and they disappeared. I can't describe how awful that was. I had no idea of where they were. … Anyway, to make a long story short, he'd brought Sam to Canada."

"Is Ev a Canadian?"

"Yes. His sister had the decency to send me a letter saying they were in Nova Scotia. She said that Sam was being looked after by a family friend during the days, when Ev was working. She didn't reply to my messages after that. But I at least knew that Sam was safe, so I felt easier."

"But why did Ev take her when he didn't have much of an appetite for being a father? Was it to punish, or hurt you?"

"Maybe … no, no, I don't think so. Ev's not like that. I

suspect his father was behind it. Everett Senior. He imagines himself to be a clan patriarch—a godfather even. His wife died giving birth to Ev so he only has the two kids of his own. His daughter has seven kids and he encouraged Ev and I to be like her. When we split up, Senior approached me with the idea of letting him adopt Sam. He even offered me a pile of money like Sam was for sale. I can only guess that he went to work on Ev and Ev complied. He's terrified of the old man. He'd gone halfway around the world to escape his influence but, well, here we are."

"How did Ev get Sam out of New Zealand without permission from you?"

"Another reason to suspect that Senior put him up to it. Senior would have no trouble getting fake paperwork, or arranging a private plane or boat."

"Is he a criminal? I mean doing something like that must require having some connections or know how."

"Senior owns the security company that was in charge at the Charlie Lawrence party ..."

"That employs the goons."

"Yes. I'm sure he knows his way around things like getting fake identities. And the fact that he employs ... goons ... who will kill ..."

"Kill?"

"... I mean, men that beat people up, tells you that just because he works in the security business doesn't mean he's always law-abiding."

"Sounds like the mob. So the goons beat you up because ..."

"Because I'm here trying to get Sam back. They want to scare me off and make me give up looking for Sam. Anyway, that's why I was at Charlie's stupid shindig. Ev used to work for his dad before I met him in New Zealand, and he'd been responsible for Charlie Lawrence's security. I wanted to see if Ev was there; back working for his dad and for Charlie. And if he was, I planned to follow him and see if he would lead me to Sam."

"Why not just approach him?"

"He's a kidnapper who snuck away. Why would he tell me

anything?"

"Have you've been to the police?"

"Of course—Sam was kidnapped—but no luck so far. I'm guessing they asked around and Ev is lying low because he knows the cops are looking for him."

"So he wasn't at the soiree?"

"I don't know. At least I didn't see him."

"You know, after you took off—when the two goons were still on the patio—I saw a man in a nice suit come out and give them orders. He was acting all pissed off and pointing in the direction of the patio opening you'd gone through."

"Just a sec ..." Vanessa took up her camera and began flipping through her saved photos. "Was it him?" she asked, holding the camera up in front of my face.

I looked closely at a photograph of a young man, tanned and wearing a Hawaiian shirt. He was a little older now but this was the guy. "I'd say so. Definitely."

"That's Ev. I wonder how I missed him."

"Well, I passed the security office door just inside the entrance. It was closed. He could have been in there."

"Maybe he spotted me on CCTV. I was trying to be discrete but you never know."

"So it was him that asked the goons to beat you up it seems."

Vanessa considered the comment. "No ... Ev wouldn't condone that. His father might have though. The goons work for him so they would have followed his orders. Ev might have just been telling them to follow me."

We sat quietly after that. I'd put our empty dishes in the sink, but we had mugs of tea in front of us.

In spite of her openness, an odd notion struck me: that Vanessa was still standing in shadow. I think it was my dramatic training. I could distinguish between actual speech and that of an actor imitating it—and her narration felt false.

When Vanessa talked about her daughter being kidnapped and her fear for the girl's safety, she'd done so in a manner that could be called dispassionate. Not what you'd expect from a desperate and scared parent.

On the other hand, I thought, maybe she'd told the story so many times that she was now just reciting words. Which might even be a purposeful way to distance herself from her feelings.

Having spent several minutes in reflection, sitting with empty mugs on the table in front of us, I asked, "So I gather you've spoken to Senior?"

"Of course. He says that Sam isn't with him and he doesn't know where she is. Said he would speak to Ev if he saw him but they have no contact. Something I now know was a lie. He urged me to go back to New Zealand and leave matters to him. He pretended to be concerned but he claimed he wanted to keep out of a domestic dispute."

"And you've spoken to the daughter? The one who said that Sam was spending the days at the house of a family friend. I'd assume that she must know what's going on."

"I'm sure she does. But she claims she doesn't."

"I heard the goons say that they'd warned you to leave. When was that?"

"They stopped me as I was leaving Senior's security company building and threatened me; told me that I needed to go home or they would take matters into their own hands."

"And you think Senior directed him to do that?"

"It's what I suspect, yeah. But I have no plans to stop looking for Sam, whatever they do."

"So what now?"

"I've taken to spying. I rented a car and secretly watched Senior's place and his daughter Wanda's. I'm now sure that Sam doesn't go there during the day or stay there at night. I've avoided checking the homes of any of Senior's extended family since Ev always told me that his father had nothing to do with them. He thought they were all 'liberal layabouts', to quote him, and he only trusts his close friends. In her letter to me, Wanda said that Sam was staying with a quote, family friend, unquote. She didn't say a friend of Ev's or hers, but a family friend, so I think she maybe let something out she didn't intend to: that Sam is with a friend of Senior's."

"Any idea of who his friends are?"

"It's hard to say, but I have a good idea. His security company's website lists three of the big accounts they handle security for. Ev once told me that Senior's largest clients are also his closest friends. In my online searches I saw pictures of Senior at charity events with the CEOs of the three companies so I marked them down as possible buddies. Started a list. Ev also said that Senior's also pretty chummy with some big name politicians. He must be since he gets government contracts to handle security for major events. I came across multiple photos of Senior with a pair of politicians so I added them to my list. After I had no luck watching Senior's and Wanda's houses I began spying on the people on my list."

"Does the list making have anything to do with why you were taking photographs at Charlie's party."

Vanessa shifted in her chair and frowned, apparently uncomfortable with either her sitting position or the question. "Partly. I always have a camera at hand. … There were so many people in the crowd that I was afraid that, even if Ev was there that I'd miss him. My plan was to go over the pics later to see if his face popped up. But yes, another reason for the photos was to document the faces of the people who were there."

"Have you gone through the photos yet?"

"I did, last night. I didn't see Ev but I now know though— since you spotted him—that he was at the party, and he's back working for Charlie Lawrence."

"I get the impression … I mean from your reactions when I mention his name, that you don't like Charlie. Why is that?"

"I went to see him to ask if Ev was back working for him. I told him my story. It didn't surprise me that he was unhelpful, since I know he's definitely pals with Senior, but what he said went beyond that. He said that if Ev took Sam that he must have had a reason … if you can imagine. He was really aggressive. Practically accused me of being an unfit mother." I recognized the loathing that came over Vanessa's face. It was the third time I'd seen it.

"So, do you think he knows where your daughter is?"

"I do. And he's covering for his buddy, Senior."

"It still seems strange to me that the goons were so aggressive."

"Me too. My guess is that Senior's worried I'll spirit Sam off if I find her. He's not used to being challenged and—if the stories Ev tells are true—his response to challenges is always a violent one. Ev tells how he was terrified of his dad as a kid and had to be careful of everything he said around him … and I think he's still afraid of him."

"So beating people up isn't necessarily a service on offer from his company."

"No, I don't think so. I assume it's only in my case, although I do think it's a possibility—again, from stuff Ev's said—that some of Senior's buddies might be into some questionable stuff."

"And you seem to think that Charlie Lawrence is one of them."

"It wouldn't surprise me. But maybe it's just the fact that I can't stomach the prick."

"I would imagine that you did a little spying on Charlie Lawrence's house since he's one of Ev's friends."

"I did. There was no one home."

"Would it help if I speak to him and ask about Ev? See if he knows anything."

"No, don't do that. If you talk to him I assume he'll give you the same story. And it may be true that he knows nothing."

As I was about ready to leave, I stopped at the doorway to the livingroom where Vanessa was sitting on the couch. "I'll come straight home after work," I said, "so I should be here by 11:30 or so."

"So you'll be at work in the glass-walled room?"

"I don't know. He sometimes eats in his suite. Plus, he doesn't stay at the hotel every day. On top of that I may get fired when I get in to work. It came out at the soiree, when I was talking to Charlie, that I'm an actor. I'm afraid that he'll not want me around anymore knowing I may associate with people his wife knows—and maybe even her."

71

"His suite? So you serve him in his apartment?"

"Sometimes."

"Let me guess. He carries on love affairs there."

I shrugged.

"Oh right. Your silence is paid for. Your lips are sealed."

I blushed, humiliated by the remark, but I managed to say, "Make yourself dinner. There's lots in the fridge. Just help yourself. Remember, there's a house and an apartment key hanging on the hooks by the door if you go out. ... Do you have any special plans for the day—if I may ask?"

"I need to go to my apartment and get some of my stuff. I have to go some time. My passport is there for one thing. I don't have much stuff but I can't just walk away from it. And I must have my laptop; it's not even mine."

"I guess it's the actor in me, and this may sound silly, but, so the goons don't nab you, you could disguise yourself. There's a blonde wig in your bedroom that Ellis got while she was working on a play last year. She cut off her hair for the role and they gave her the wig she used in the early scenes." Eyeing Vanessa up and down I added, surprised by the realization, "You know, with the wig and one of the pairs of sunglasses that Ellis keeps on her dresser, to hide your dark eyebrows, you could actually pass as her. ... I mean, from a bit of a distance."

Vanessa smiled indulgently. "I might do that." She stood up. "I have a request. Can I use your WI-fi after I get my laptop?"

"Of course. I'll write down the password and all that. Oh, and I'll leave my phone her in case you need it."

Soon after, having rushed down the apartment stairs to avoid my landlady, I set out for my theatre group meeting.

I felt more satisfied than I had for the last seventeen hours now that I had some answers about what had happened at Charlie's soiree. I had the sense though, that there was more to it then what I knew.

Stage Direction for the theatrical version of _Playing With Shadows_.

To be read in a voice-over and accompanied by stills from _The Secret_, projected onto the stage screen.

Segment of a theatre review of The Secret, posted on the blog of Eléonore Brunette, a local filmmaker.

There is a wonderful literary tradition among our finest story-tellers. They tell the stories of people who live in the shadows. Those whose voices are never heard. The Willy Lomans of the world. And more often than not, these are stories of folks who are generally viewed with contempt.

The tradition is as old as Mark Twain's novel featuring a slave and a white boy— who would have been commonly referred to as 'white trash'—travelling down the Mississippi River. And it's as new as films like _Moonlight_ and _The Florida Project_ where a gay drug dealer and a woman who turns to prostitution to support her daughter, respectively, are treated sympathetically.

This is a tradition of storytelling—of giving voice to the voiceless—that we need now more than ever. But with a difference. We are now aware that people are fully able to tell their own stories and that those who have been silenced, includes almost the entirety of women and minorities.

We need to hear their stories, told in their

own words, especially in these divisive times.

Just listen to that frat boy on Fox News, who's likely never been out of his own gated neighbourhood, and the other paid whores on the network trying to spin reality to instill fear and to help elect those whose only concern is the ultra-wealthy and corporations.

All stories are about loneliness. We exchange stories to sate our curiosity about others and to let them know us. And this builds community and peace. Without a diversity of stories and story tellers we are left afraid of each other, existing on a diet of self-serving corporate myths, and the false consolation of false love stories.

This is why I am so appreciative of recent initiatives like the new play entitled *The Secret*, staged by a fledgling company of recent Halifax theatre graduates.

The Secret is about a Syrian refugee family, as conceived by one of the members of The Other Theatre: Hassan Seleh. A Syrian refugee himself, Seleh plays the lead role and members of his actual family play the parts of the character's stage family. So it's a personal story—although fictionalized—told by individuals based on their own experiences.

The other members of the theatre company —who wrote their own parts—portray non Syrian characters and reflect a variety of social attitudes to refugees.

The existence of The Other Theatre is a testament to the fact that not only do the lessons of the last decade tell us that the entertainment industry needs to be diversified—so that people who have been

74

shut out will now have a voice—but that the problems with the current industry are largely an outcome of its structure, of who controls it, and its limits to inclusion because of the cost of production. We need reform but we also need alternatives to the current industries.

The Secret is an example of what can be done outside of such an industry. The play tells a community story and it can be set in community locations not intended to stage theatre. Plus there is pay-what-you-can ticket pricing so everyone can attend. In various ways *The Secret* doesn't set out to create a fixed commodity since the actors can change their lines and even scenes from performance to performance. And since it includes music, photography, and film from Syrian culture, what constitutes theatre is also wide open.

The Other Theatre's first production *The Secret* was staged, three months after our spring graduation, in the rented basement of a local church.

We—the theatre company members I mean—considered the play to have been a success by every measure.

We'd plastered the downtown with posters so there was a good turn-out for every performance. And the critical response was uniformly positive.

The person most responsible for the production was Hassan Seleh. He devised the plot and starred as Nizar, the patriarch of a Syrian refugee family. A trained physician in Syria, Nizar was working as a taxi driver in Halifax. Although the play showed the disparate levels of adjustment the family members had made, the play focused on Nizar's story.

The secret in question referred to an incident that occurred to Nizar late one evening. He had lashed out while being robbed on the street and as a result of that a young man lay in the hospital in a coma. In spite of suffering from PTSD, Nizar felt that he couldn't go to the police, based on his negative experience with them during a previous encounter, and he feared his family's status in the country could be jeopardized. Keeping the secret, trying to hide in the shadows as the police zeroed in, wreaked havoc with him, his family, and his faith.

Hassan was now living in Toronto, attending graduate school, so our next play would mean a much different role for the remaining five members of The Other Theatre.

Four of us members were recent university graduates who'd studied acting: myself, Lumina, Isadora, and Kevin. The other member was Dag, who we'd connected with at Casey's Pub. He'd just finished a college diploma in video and film production, and also had a degree in sound production. He was working at the city's massive new convention centre; a huge space with a state of the art sound system. Dag was thrilled to have been entrusted with it.

All five of us had co-written and acted in *The Secret* and we expected to do the same for our next production.

I felt blessed to be part of a group with four exceptionally talented others.

The afternoon meeting of The Other Theatre company was to begin at 2:00 PM in the basement of Kevin Darrow's parents' house.

Their family room was large, which would allow the five of us to sit in a circle on folding chairs the same as we'd done while workshopping *The Secret*.

As I'd walked to the Darrow house, my thoughts were on anything but our future play. Instead, I was wondering about the feasibility of planting a recording device in Charlie Lawrence's private dining room within the restaurant. I'd looked up the devices online, shortly before leaving home, and discovered that they were readily available and inexpensive.

It was Isadora—since she was the one who'd taken the lead in organizing the meeting—who kicked things off. "I think it's safe to say that we're going to miss Hassan but I want to remind everyone that, although we were recruited and organized by him, specifically to work on *The Secret*, that we are all trained and creative individuals capable of putting together something just as compelling as that play. We all contributed our ideas to *The Secret* and wrote our own parts. It was a success—I think—because it was a truly collaborative effort."

"Agreed," said Lumina, sitting to Isadora's right.

"I have," Isadora continued, "made a list of the characteristics of out first production thinking that we could retain or reject any of these in our second effort."

She began by mentioning the mixed-media approach we'd taken, and the inclusion of both real and fictional elements. She went on to say, "Our subject matter was local … or, at least, provincial. The story was suspenseful. We had minimal sets. And each of us took on multiple roles. ... I'm sure someone will let me know if I missed anything important. The question is: do we duplicate all of those features in our next play?"

"I think so," said Kevin. Always restless and full of energy he'd gotten up at the beginning of the meeting and was standing behind his chair, leaning on the back of it. "I also recall that, right after the play wrapped, at the debrief, that we said that all our plays should focus on political issues."

"I like the idea of continuing in that direction," said Isadora, nodding her head. "Does everyone agree?"

Various people voiced their assent.

"I'm okay if we do something political, or if we don't," Dag said, "but I think we should choose a story—or maybe an issue—that is current and affects us directly."

"I agree," said Kevin. "*The Secret* originated with one of our members and reflected his community. And he recruited other people from that community. I think it's fitting that we always do that. Like what Eléonore Brunette said in her review: people are capable of telling their own stories so we shouldn't try to tell the stories of others but to tell our own."

After coming to a general agreement on our approach to the new play, and to do something that was 'current, local, personal, and political', in Isadora's words, she went around the room, calling on each of us, in turn, to present a story idea.

Kevin wanted to set the play in a seniors home, with every character reflecting some aspect of aging. "It could be physical, like losing the ability to do things the person used to be able to do. Memory loss is common. There's retirement boredom and invisibility. There's ... I don't know ... the presumption of wisdom. And there's the romantic fascination with someone who's a lot younger: idealization."

"Jesus," said Dag, "that's all we need, another Lolita. These days it would just come off as disgusting, like watching some old codger fiddling with himself in the park."

That objection—on top of the fact that none of us were

seniors—led to Kevin's idea getting the thumbs down.

Isadora was next up and suggested that we set the play in the 1960's, in a converted school bus with a bunch of hippie folk singers travelling to a folk festival.

The idea had some potential since both Isadora and Lumina were also musicians, so could perform any music in the play. On the down side, doing a musical might lead to logistical problems. As far as story angles went, one could imagine that there would be dramatic tension from romantic entanglements. Most significant though was that the musicians, like us, would be people just beginning their careers in the arts industry so their struggles would reflect our own. It could thus be considered to be about current issues despite the historical setting. Plus, it would check the box of doing a play that reflected our personal stories.

We moved on from the folk singer idea without making a firm decision about it one way or the other.

As the meeting progressed I'd become increasingly worried about what I would say when it became my turn to present an idea. We'd agreed at Casey's, several days before, that we'd all show up today with at least one plot suggestion but I'd put off developing anything, thinking that I'd have time to do so a day or two before the meeting. Problem was, I'd been unexpectedly distracted over the weekend.

When my turn came, I said, "I was thinking about hidden devices that can record people." I shifted uncomfortably in my chair with no idea of what to say next having not rehearsed my pitch. I was aware that everyone's eyes were focused expectantly on me. I continued, "Lumina and I work in a restaurant and we could secretly record the conversations of diners. The play could be based on the most interesting and compelling stories we hear."

"So you mean, we secretly record people and then play the recordings?" Lumina asked.

"I'm thinking we re-enact them," I began, thinking out load. "The stage could be dark and only one restaurant table at a time illuminated. Each of us can sit at a table with another person or two. When our table is in the spotlight, we present a story in our character's life. After each episode the

79

lights can dim and we can move around to play secondary parts at other tables."

Lumina frowned. "Is that even legal, to secretly record people? Don't we need people's permission?"

Defensively, I said, "We wouldn't include the actual tape recordings, like I said. And we would change things up a bit."

"But if people recognize their conversation and where they said certain things, couldn't they sue the restaurant for, I don't know, invasion of privacy or something … and you … and us?"

I wanted to agree with Lumina, and would have had anyone else come up with such an idiotic idea, but I took a shot at defending it nonetheless. "Wouldn't we just be doing what reporters do, or detectives?"

Lumina countered, "Yes, and the circumstances might justify it, but reporters sometimes cross the line. When I lived in Toronto there was a case where some Muslim girls were murdered by their parents for that whole defending their honour nonsense. At the trial there was photographic evidence from one of the dead girls; phone selfies she'd taken in the bathroom. She was in her underwear. Just a teenage girl exploring her own sexuality. But one of the newspapers printed the photos. The reporter—Rosie something or other—said it was what the young woman would have wanted. But Rosie couldn't know that since she didn't even know the person! The young woman had kept her pictures private so showing them was a gross invasion of her privacy; the exploitation of someone's personal life."

"I don't like the idea of exploiting people," said Kevin. He'd recently taken up nervous pacing but was now standing in a far corner.

"Nor I," said Isadora, who even provided us with a critical digression on an artist named Sophie Calle whose early art consisted of violations of privacy, like getting a job as a chambermaid and then photographing people's private things, as if their lives were just there for her to exploit.

I felt a bit chagrined but couldn't disagree when my suggestion was axed. Lumina and the others were undoubtedly correct.

I consoled myself with the thought that there were times when secret surveillance might be acceptable—to stop an act of terrorism or to find a kidnapped child—if the investigation was targeted and not a sweeping violation of privacy. But commercializing some random person's life without permission had no justification.

I wondered if maybe the issue of surveillance versus privacy could be turned into the subject of our play but no immediate plot idea sprang to mind.

We kicked things around a bit without settling on a subject for the next play. Nothing came of Lumina's idea that we take a page from early post-modern film and depict a single incident over and over; each according to how one participant remembered it so that each version differed from all the others. It had become a commonplace approach. It was a sticky decision to reject the suggestion because Isadora pointed out that it was what we were doing to some extent when we presented different voices as we'd done in *The Secret*.

In the end, there was a consensus agreement to continue the process of coming up with story ideas but to discuss them online rather than at another meeting. We would email each other with our suggestions and comment on what we received.

"The key thing," Isadora said, as a final word on what our task ahead was, "is to tell your own story."

I arrived at work fifteen minutes before the start of my 4:30 PM shift.

Lumina was already there. "Mr. Lawrence and a guest will be here at 7:30 for dinner," she told me, efficiently. She always spoke formally in work situations when others were present. "The table has already been set." She then hustled off, busy with the task of preparing everyone and everything for dinner service since she was acting as supervisor during the manager's vacation.

I was relieved. Nothing had changed. All afternoon I'd been increasingly stressed about the possibility of losing my job. Not just because I'd miss Charlie's tips but because I would have no chance of seeing or hearing something that might help Vanessa in her search for her daughter Sam.

Charlie Lawrence, with a male friend in tow, didn't arrive for dinner until five minutes before eight.

I recognized the guest's face—a forty-something man in a suit who'd been there before—but I didn't know his name.

Charlie, as always, was solicitous and friendly—at first. Usually, soon after he and his guests were seated, I became part of the furniture, but tonight when I was pouring the wine, Charlie said, "So Pete, I was surprised to hear that you're an actor. How come you never mentioned it?"

"I didn't want you to think I was angling for acting work, Mr. Lawrence."

"Very commendable. Are you working anywhere at the moment?"

I told him about belonging to a new theatre company and that we were planning another original production.

"Really? How interesting," Charlie said. "Have you set a budget yet?"

"We haven't gotten that far. We're just getting started."

"Yes, of course. Will you rent a performance space?"

"Yes, but I don't know where."

"A larger space will announce that your group is a serious one. What's your advertising plan?"

I again responded that things were still in early stages and this hadn't been discussed. "At this point we haven't even decided on what the subject of the play will be."

"Well, when you've firmed things up a bit we should talk. I might even be able to make some suggestions before that, if you're interested. I recall now that I heard about your last play. It was obviously well done and you sound like a very talented ensemble. You'll need some funding if you want to step up your game though. I'd consider providing that. It would be an investment worth making. Most artists are so bound up with their craft that they forget they're producing a product for public consumption. With decent funding you could reach a much larger audience in a bigger theatre and have a longer run—even bring in a top-flight director like Jeff Weir."

I mumbled a thank you and said I'd speak to my group.

That seemed to satisfy Charlie because he ignored me for the rest of the dinner. Normalcy had been restored.

Throughout the rest of my work shift, I wondered how I could explain to The Other Theatre members that Charlie Lawrence wanted to invest in our little theatre group.

They would no doubt wonder why the guy would invest in something so small time and I certainly wasn't about to explain that it was a bribe to keep me from telling anyone about his personal life.

By the end of my shift I'd decided to say nothing to my friends about Charlie's proposal.

I recalled his statement: 'I might even be able to make some suggestions'. It was clear from the way that he'd pitched his offer that he thought of all theatre as just another product, like hamburger or tires, and that bigger was better. There was no way I could sanction Charlie having a voice in what we did. It would defeat the whole purpose of The Other Theatre: to let people who weren't always standing in the light a forum to tell their own stories in their own voices. Charlie couldn't be part of an alternative when he was the norm that we were trying to be an alternative to.

The only thing I now had to consider was how to tell Charlie Lawrence—without telling him what I thought of his productions—why I wasn't interested in his financing offer.

I went straight home after work rather than to Casey's, knowing that Vanessa would have been by herself all day. I felt a pang of regret about not getting to see Stacey.

The office chair in Ellis's room could be heard moving the moment I opened the apartment door.

Whether it was from loneliness or anxiousness to tell me about something, Vanessa had clearly been listening for me. I shook my shoes off at the door and looked up to see her a few feet away, waiting. Despite appearing exhausted, she smiled and launched into a report on her day.

"Thanks for the loan of your phone," she began, then proceeded to tell me about the call she'd made to her landlady, Mrs. Page, immediately after I'd left that morning. "I didn't go into specifics when I spoke to her but I stuck to the truth—sort of. I explained that the men who came to her door weren't Immigration agents but stalkers who'd tracked me down, and I wanted to avoid them. It was obvious, from the way she talked, that she'd inferred that one of them was an ex boyfriend and I didn't correct her. The story got her up in arms. I wasn't surprised when she said she'd help me. It's something I've noticed about a lot of old ladies. You'd think that they'd be the people most afraid of violent men because they're practically helpless, physically speaking, but the reality—from the stuff I saw back home—is that they're fearless and stand up for young women. Anyway, Mrs. Page went to her window and saw the goons sitting in front of her house in a car. She wanted to call the police but I convinced her to just let me in the back door so I could get some things —that calling the cops would inflame the situation and put me in more danger."

I was impressed with Vanessa's ability to weave a convincing story on the fly, and told her so.

She reddened and said, "Oh, and just to be on the safe side, I also took your suggestion and disguised myself with Ellis's wig and sunglasses before I went out. When I got off the bus in Dartmouth I walked by my street, along the block south of it, and saw Senior's goons still camped out in front."

"Did you meet my dear Mrs. Tate coming or going?" I asked.

"No, I didn't see her at all, but then again, I didn't look for her."

Vanessa had retrieved her laptop from the apartment she'd been staying in and told me that she'd spent the day researching online.

"Any luck?" I asked.

"No, and I'm getting frustrated." Vanessa's tone reinforced her words. "I seem to be going in circles. My focus has been on constructing the web of friendships around Senior ..."

"Because Ev's sister said that Sam was staying with a family friend and you assume it's a friend of Senior's."

"Exactly. But I've run up against a wall. The same few names keep coming up again and again, and I've checked out all of their places. The logical next step, if I stay on the same track, will be to try to build a web of friends of the family friends."

"So one of the family friends may have a daughter, for example, and Sam is with her."

"That's the idea, yes. But I'm running out of time and that's a needle in a haystack sort of approach. I was just thinking before you got home that I should go back to the beginning and look for Ev. To focus on him."

"But you had no luck with that, you said. Do you have any new ideas about where he might be staying?"

"Not yet. The only thing I know for certain about him—or at least I think I do—is that he's back working for Charlie Lawrence. So looking for Ev means focusing on Charlie."

"Okay, and how do you do that?"

"Well, I know nothing about Charlie's business. It sounds like a mini entertainment empire ..."

"Not far off."

"I assume that Senior's company is getting all of Charlie's business so I want to build a list of all the places he might need security for. I can then check them out. I think those will will be the places where Ev might show up during the daytime. Like Charlie's hotel. His office. His … what? The theatres that he operates out of? Other stuff. … Can I pick your brain?"

I agreed but made sure that Vanessa knew that I was anything but an expert on Charlie Lawrence's business empire. Even so, she said, I probably knew a lot more than her, and maybe a lot more than I realized.

So, for the next hour, I did most of the talking while Vanessa asked questions and took notes.

Vanessa was right, I did know more than I thought I did; stuff you pick up by a sort of cultural osmosis I suppose. I came up with a fairly long list of the theatre productions Charlie had produced and some of the musical acts he'd brought into the city. I hit a wall though, when it came to the film and television stuff he'd been involved in. Of those, I knew nothing."

"I should be able to find that stuff online," Vanessa said. "And that might help me to pinpoint some locations."

"Charlie ate at the restaurant tonight," I said. "I don't know if knowing this will be of any value to you but he had a male guest. I knew the guy's face because he's been at the restaurant a few times, but I had no idea of who he is. Anyway, I asked Lumina about him and she said his name is Brian Hemmings and that he's Charlie's comptroller. It's probably nothing."

"Maybe, but who knows. I'll see if I can find an address for him. If I can, I'll have a look at his place—or at least my version of Ellis will."

"Do you have a car?" I asked. "Sounds like you've had to get around a lot."

"I've rented them."

"My mother has a little car that she lets me borrow anytime I want. She almost never uses it. If you get some more names and addresses of places that Sam might be I can escort you around or just let you take the car."

"That would be amazing. I'm running out of money. Thanks!"

"I'll call her first thing in the morning."

"I can drive the car, like you said. I have an international driver's license." Vanessa appeared to be self-conscious as she explained, "I'd rather drive myself because I'll want to check houses when you're at work, in the late evening, because it's dark. I like to go then because I can get up close to windows for some Peeping Tom work."

"I'm fine with you driving," I said, thinking that Vanessa's approach sounded dangerous and maybe not the best one given that, late at night, small kids would be in bed, in darkened rooms.

"Great. First off, I want to re-visit Charlie Lawrence's house in the country. I didn't see anyone the day I was there but I gather his wife lives at the house. ... Is that right?"

"So far as I know."

"If Sam's there, then the wife will be the one looking after her."

"I can't guarantee the car will be available but I'll check first thing."

On reflection, Charlie's wife Addison didn't strike me as someone who would wish to be consigned to babysitting duty. She struck me as pure princess. But then again, I thought, what did I know about her ... or about babysitting for that matter.

I told Vanessa about my idea to plant a recording device at Charlie's private dining room and how I'd rejected it after getting shot down at the afternoon meeting of The Other Theatre members; the reason being that it was an illegal and unethical thing to do. I asked her what she thought of it.

"It's something to consider. Let me think about it. I believe in protecting people's privacy, like your friends say, but, like you, I think there may be circumstances that justify it. I'm just not sure of where the line is and when it's okay to cross it."

Tuesday.

I got up at 7:30 AM, after the first ring of my alarm, and immediately phoned my mother. I told her that I had a friend from New Zealand visiting for several days and wanted to show her around.

Mom was happy to let me take her car on an open-ended basis but needed it for most of the day. I said I would swing by her building after work, on my way home, and get the car from the parking lot where she kept it. She'd sold the family home a year before and bought a condo in a seniors building because it was well situated with stores nearby that she could walk to.

"I'll call you if I absolutely need to borrow the car back," Mom said. "At most, if I need it, it'll only be for a morning."

Shortly after the phone call, I set out for a nearby grocery store to buy some milk for breakfast.

I had just started up the stairs to my flat, on my return, when the dreaded Mrs. Tate came shooting through her apartment door like she'd been sprung from a Howitzer.

She called my name and I reluctantly stopped on the stairs and turned to face the music which was bound to be unpleasant. Mrs. Tate said sternly. "I saw you go out yesterday and after that, all through the day and the evening, I could hear the floor crunching from someone walking around."

I stared blankly back at her.

"Ellis told me that she was going away so it sounds like someone else is living with you. It's none of my business who you have there, God knows there's no one who respects other people's privacy like I do, but I just wanted to remind you that your rent is based on a two person occupancy and extra money will be required if a third party is living there, like a boyfriend or girlfriend."

Now, there's no way that the existence of a full-time occupant could reasonably be inferred from the noises of a single day. I guessed that the reason for Mrs. Tate's ambush was simply that she was burning to know what was happening upstairs.

I hesitated. Vanessa was hiding out and I didn't want anyone to know she was staying with me. I needed a story. "No Mrs. Tate, it's just Ellis." As soon as the words were out of my mouth, I started to chastise himself. Why hadn't I gone with the story I'd told my mother, that a friend from New Zealand was staying with me for a week? Instead, I'd told a stupid, easily disprovable lie, likely because Vanessa had disguised herself as Ellis the day before.

"So her tour fell through?"

"No, she just came back for a couple of days."

The trouble with lies is that they multiply like bunnies, needing new lies to explain the old ones.

I turned and marched up the rest of the stairs.

Struggling for words, Mrs. Tate said, "That … it's …"

I closed the apartment door behind me and stood still, listening to her muttering to herself and eventually retreating into her unit. Stupid, stupid, I thought. I slipped my shoes off and mulled over my story, trying to put a positive spin on things and escape the self-recrimination. Maybe Mrs. Tate had seen Vanessa leaving or arriving the day before, dressed as Ellis. I was just going with the deception that was already in play, and affirming it. But the relief from beating myself up was brief. I hadn't seen Vanessa in her Ellis disguise but I suspected that it would only fool someone who didn't know Ellis and had only seen her from a distance. One good close-up glimpse of the blonde woman, by Mrs. Tate, would be enough for her to know that she wasn't Ellis.

"You're going to have to sprint up and down the apartment stairs," I said, as soon as Vanessa appeared in the hallway.

She stopped and waited for an explanation.

I went on to explain what had just transpired between myself and Mrs. Tate. I concluded the story with, "Maybe, when she realizes I lied to her, she'll think I'm involved in some sort of criminal activity and that could make things even more complicated."

Vanessa laughed. It was clear that my lie didn't rate very

high on her list of things to worry about. With a 1940's movie accent, said, "Don't worry your pretty little head about it honey. It'll be fine."

I'd convinced Vanessa that it would be easier if she just accepted my hospitality and forgot about buying her own food. She seemed genuinely reluctant to accept the offer but eventually agreed.

We were in the kitchen, making breakfast, moving about, dodging each other in the small space, when I advised Vanessa that I wouldn't be getting my mother's car until the next day.

She did her best to hide her disappointment but without much success. "It may turn out to be for the best," she said, possibly for my benefit, like I shouldn't feel bad for failing to get the car. "I found an address for Brian Hemmings' house and looked it up online. Walking there will be no problem. I can watch to see if Ev shows up. And, also, to see if Sam is staying there."

"Well, be careful," I said. "I hope you'll go as Ellis. I don't want you getting grabbed by any more security goons. ... I can't hit anyone with a boulder if I'm not there."

She smiled. "Not to worry. I'll keep my eyes open. Plus, I'll be here most of the day, so I'm safe."

"I was thinking about that on my walk home last night, wondering whether they could track you down."

"I don't see how they could. They can't link me to you since I stood in the shadows at the soiree, even if they look at the CCTV."

"Maybe, if they have CCTV footage, they'll see me heading into the corner of the patio where you were standing, then walking towards the bush trail where you were attacked."

"I see you're worried. Sorry. But I don't see how they could know where on the patio I was. And a lot of people on the patio were going out to the smoking area and back. All I can say is, please don't worry about it overly much. You said that no one there knew you and that you were there under a false name. Even if they spot you on the CCTV they have no way of knowing who you are or where you live. You're safe."

Unless they show the footage to Charlie, I thought, which might happen if they decide that I was the man who likely came to Vanessa's aid.

Shortly after lunch I was sitting at the desk in my bedroom when Vanessa presented herself in the doorway with a "Ta da."

I looked up. She was wearing one of Ellis's outfits, sporting her blonde wig and a pair of her sunglasses. Her resemblance to Ellis was astonishing!

"I have a plan," Vanessa said with a grin, seemingly enjoying my incredulity. "I'm going to wait at the apartment door until it's quiet downstairs. I'll then make like a sprinter so I can get out the door before the old lady downstairs can stop me. Hopefully, she'll be at her front window and will see me leave. I have my own clothes in this old Sobey's bag I found in Ellis's room. Before I come back, I'll change into them, and become me again. I'll make sure the old lady sees me when I get back here. Maybe I'll make a show of looking at a piece of paper to make sure I have the right house before I come up the walk and into the house. You can then tell her that Ellis is gone and Vanessa has arrived."

One again I marvelled at Vanessa's ability to quickly concoct a story. I said, "That's brilliant. Maybe, if Mrs. Tate confronts you, you could tell her that you're my cousin, here for a visit."

Vanessa smiled at my concern. "Don't you worry, I'll spin her a lovely yarn if I happen to meet her."

I watched Vanessa from the front window.

When she got to the sidewalk out front she slowly paraded past the front of the house. Damn, she looked like Ellis, I thought. Mrs. Tate must have been at her spot by the front window because Vanessa did a quick nod and wave in that direction. The new Ellis had left the building.

As I watched her walk along the sidewalk, I considered her plan to spy on Brian Hemmings' house.

It made sense, to me, that Ev might show up at any of the places where Charlie conducted business, to check on security there or whatever it was he did. I wasn't convinced though that his employees would also be covered by whatever security arrangement he had with Senior's company. And I thought the possibility that Sam was staying with the Hemmings was even more unlikely. By definition, an employee of Charlie's was a different thing than a friend of Charlie's. I didn't say these things to Vanessa. My guess was that they'd occurred to her but that she was desperate and willing to test every possible option for finding Ev or Sam.

Who knows, I thought hopefully, she could be right to do so.

"So what happened to you last night?" Lumina asked almost immediately after I'd checked into work for my shift. There was no one else around so she'd slipped into familiar mode. "I went looking for you after work but Davy told me you'd already left."

"Sorry, I forgot to mention it yesterday. My cousin is in town for a couple of weeks and staying with me. It was a last minute thing. I only found out about it Friday night. She'd planned to travel with a couple of her friends but the trip fell through and she decided to come on her own so I suggested she stay with me to save money by cancelling her hotel reservation. All through my shift I was imagining her sitting around my apartment staring at the walls, so I rushed home."

"Of course, as you should have. You should have brought her to Casey's."

"I would have but she was pretty exhausted after her flight from New Zealand."

"Not surprisingly. … Oh, by the way, Charlie will be having dinner in the restaurant with a single guest tonight."

I was surprised that the dinner guest in question turned out to be Brian Hemmings. It was unusual but not the first time that Charlie had the same dinner guest two nights in a row. Whenever that happened I always assumed that he and his guest were working intently on some large project in Charlie's suite, or his office a couple of blocks away, and slipping over for dinner.

To my relief, Charlie didn't resume our conversation about funding for The Other Theatre. I hadn't yet decided how to phrase my negative response.

Charlie nodded at me when I first entered his glass dining room, and said, "Hi Pete," as usual. But it was a subdued effort; not the collegial pose he usually effected.

The night before I'd been relieved about the call to serve Charlie dinner, both because I relied on the tip money and because it was an opportunity of maybe overhearing something that would help Vanessa. But looking at Charlie on this night, and realizing that he was somehow complicit in the kidnapping of a child, served to eclipse those earlier feelings. I was repulsed by being in his presence and knew that I could soon no longer justify working for him. I decided that once Vanessa's problem was resolved, that I'd resign.

My grim future played through my thoughts throughout my shift. Leaving the job had some downsides that I'd have to face, but that was unavoidable. Whatever job I got next would pay less—so would likely mean longer hours. And I might have trouble getting time off for my theatre work. Mr. Skelton, the restaurant manager at the hotel, was supportive of Lumina's and my ambitions to act, and he'd given us a few days to work on *The Secret*. But I wouldn't know with a new boss—not until I needed the time off—how he or she would react. I couldn't see going into an interview and telling someone that they couldn't rely on me.

I'd gotten spoiled and was now facing the dilemmas and financial uncertainty that most of my theatre friends faced.

After work, I walked to my mother's place, and since she'd be sleeping at that time of night, I went directly to the indoor parking lot where she kept her car. The condo was only two blocks from Stacey's apartment.

Stacey would likely be at the pub at that time of night, I reflected, and she likely would have been there the evening before as well. I wondered if she'd be wondering what had became of me since I stopped at Casey's every weeknight. I wished that I could drop into the pub and explain. Make sure she didn't think that I was avoiding her. But I felt that I needed to get home to check on Vanessa. Alas.

I drove to my place and was forced to park up the street because there were too many cars lining the curb in front of the house.

We were sitting in my livingroom as short time later when Vanessa said, with a stoic look, "I found the Hemmings' house, but there was no sign of either Ev or Sam."

"How long were you there?"

"A couple of hours. I saw a woman—Brian's wife I assume—leave in a car. The place was quiet after that until lunch when I saw a couple of kids come home and then leave an hour or so later."

"Where did you watch from?"

"There's a little parkette across the street where I could sit without drawing any notice and a couple of times I circled the block to look into the backyard. I saw no one. In the afternoon I went downtown and wandered around the theatre where you said Charlie stages most of his plays. I saw no sign of Ev."

"Sorry. Oh, I got my mother's car and it's parked up the street."

"That's great! Thank you. Tomorrow I'll check out the Lawrence house."

"So how did it go with Mrs. Tate? Did you pull off your ruse on your return trip? You did a nice job on your departure. I should recruit you to The Other Theatre."

Vanessa didn't return my smile. "Everything went according to plan," she said flatly.

"So Ellis has returned to her tour and my cousin Vanessa has now arrived for a visit."

"She's here, in the flesh."

But the fact that she was unhappier than before—and could be slipping into depression—was obvious.

It was going on for 12:30 AM when Vanessa asked if I'd be up to going for a walk. "I'm going stir crazy," she said, "in spite of my little jaunt today. I've been on my laptop all evening. I have a headache from looking at that little screen."

I was happy to oblige and felt a twinge of guilt, that I hadn't thought to suggest the idea myself. Vanessa had been sitting around the apartment for most of the last couple of days by herself.

"Will the old lady be at her window?" she asked.

"No. She's done her surveillance by 11:00."

To my surprise, Vanessa donned her trench coat and Ellis's blonde wig before we started down the house stairs. She also wore one of her fedoras. Three more of them had appeared on the rack by the front door the day before, retrieved from her apartment. It now looked like the costume department for an Indiana Jones film.

"I was wondering about something, if you don't mind me asking," Vanessa said, after we started off along the sidewalk. "It's just idle curiosity. I was wondering—because we were speaking about Charlie having dinner with his mistresses up in his room ..."

"Yes."

"What about secrecy? He's paying you to keep his secrets, but if he parades through the hotel with his mistress, everyone will see them together, which would blow his cover."

"I've heard that he picks her up in his car. I've never seen

97

her in the hotel so they use Charlie's private entrance."

"You're kidding me. He has his own entrance to the hotel? Private entrance, private server ..."

"Yeah, it's at the back of the hotel. There's a couple of loading docks for receiving—on the main floor. Beside the docks there's a ramp leading down to a basement level garage door where he parks his car. I was talking to Jimmy the receiver one day and he said that the garage door entrance is for Charlie's exclusive use. Jimmy said that Charlie's part of the basement is done up quite fancy. There's a parking space for his Porsche and some glass doors that lead to a private elevator ..."

"A private elevator too! There's a guy with nothing to hide."

"It only has three stops. The basement, the main floor, and the penthouse suite. The door on the main floor is kept locked but I have a key for it. I also have a key for Charlie's suite for that matter. Me and the manager. I was given access to them so I can get up to Charlie's suite when he's having dinner there." I stopped myself from saying more, embarrassed at the realization that I was bragging about the responsibility I'd been given to operate within Charlie's secret world and to keep what I saw to myself. It was nothing to congratulate myself for. I was inclined now to think that it was quite the opposite.

"So he sneaks his girlfriends in and out of the hotel."

"That's my theory. Jimmy said that Charlie's hyper-paranoid about privacy. There's two security cameras out back, one above the receiving dock and the other above Charlie's garage door, but that one's apparently disabled. Jimmy knows about Charlie's mistresses—he's the one who told me that Charlie picks the women up and drops them off in his car when they visit—and he thinks the second camera is turned off so no one can record his comings and goings. Jimmy said that the secrecy measures are so effective that he's never even seen one of the women."

"Neat. So if Charlie's suite is the penthouse, how many floors is this hotel?"

"Only six, but the top floor is Charlie's."

"Exclusively?"

"Well sort of. Well, no, I guess it's all his. Half the floor is his suite and the other half is a large patio that faces the ocean. It's the tallest building on the street so at least for now there's no prying eyes."

"Well thought out, Charlie."

"Indeed."

We walked in silence for a block or so before I said, "If you don't mind me asking, have you always lived in New Zealand?"

"Yes."

"How did Ev happen to be there?"

"He was travelling the world. He told me that he was trying to get away from his family. It was his father he was escaping from, really. The old man's a control freak apparently. His son and his daughter were home-schooled and it was pure indoctrination."

"About what kind of things?"

"A particular brand of hellfire and brimstone Christianity laced with extreme right wing ideology apparently. After Ev's so-called schooling, Daddy pushed him into the family security business with the idea that he'd take it over in due time. Ev hated it. He decided that he needed to find his own way and snuck off to the other side of the world. Escape the cult as it were. I suppose you're wondering how I ever got together with someone like him."

"It did cross my mind. To steal your daughter from you is pretty heartless."

"Yes, there's that, but like I said, I think it's really Senior pulling the strings. Shows how strong his control still is. Given Ev's background, it horrifies me that Sam is here, and part of that family, and possibly being indoctrinated into the same views that Ev was. … Needless to say, Ev wasn't always like he is now. He's changed over the last couple of years. I think he's come back into the old man's orbit for some reason."

"Where did you meet?"

"He was the concierge in the building where I worked."

"So, still in the security business."

"Right, at the lowest level. It was just a way to make some money while he travelled around the world. He seemed happy with the idea of staying in New Zealand after we got together. I was just starting out as a teacher but I made enough money for the two of us."

"So you got married and had Sam?"

"Yes. Things seemed fine at first but Ev worked nights and I worked days. Eventually we hardly ever saw each other. We kept Sam in daycare so Ev could sleep during the day. Out of the blue though, he quit his job one day, saying he wanted to find another one. So Sam stayed in daycare. And that was really the beginning of the end. Ev didn't do much job searching. He hung out with his friends. It was like he wanted to live all the teenage stuff he'd been denied. It was something I hadn't seen in him before. Or at least I hadn't registered it."

"You said that he wasn't especially interested in Sam …"

"Yes, and I came to realize that he'd only said that he wanted to have a kid because Senior was leaning on him. What he really wanted to do was be a kid himself and hang out with his buddies, and maybe have a girlfriend. Eventually I told him to leave if he wasn't going to look for a job and he moved out."

"And he didn't spend much time with Sam after he left."

"Right. I mean, almost none at all. He started repeating this line about how he was trying to find out who he was and that was his priority. I'd point out to him that who he was was Sam's father and my husband but it changed nothing. This went on for two years. … Well you know what happened next. One day he took Sam—supposedly for one of his whirlwind visits—and then they were gone."

"I can't imagine the stress of that. What he did is despicable for so many reasons."

We'd been walking in the direction of Stacey's apartment. As we went past her building I wondered if the direction we'd taken had been an unconscious decision on my part.

I suggested to Vanessa that we head home, so we turned and were retracing our route when I saw Stacey approaching.

As we came fact to face, I smiled and slowed. Stacey

smiled back at me and said "Hi." I responded in kind, as did Vanessa, but Stacey didn't stop to talk.

Vanessa and I half turned and watched her go, then turned back. Vanessa glanced my way—checking my reaction—but said nothing.

After Stacey went by, I felt a rush of anxiety. Just an hour or so earlier I'd been wishing that I could explain to her why I hadn't been round to the pub. Now, in all likelihood, her seeing me with Vanessa would serve as an explanation. Not only might Stacey conclude that I wasn't interested in her, but that I was seeing someone else. I felt frantic with the thought that she may have felt embarrassed and self-conscious when she saw me, and that was the reason she'd kept walking when we saw each other. Going in the direction of her place had been a stupid oversight.

I wondered whether I would ever have the chance to explain to Stacey what had been happening in my life this past week. I might just get a cold shoulder when we next met.

I hated being neurotic like this and since there was nothing I could do at that moment, I tried to console myself with the thought that I didn't need to explain anything. Walking with someone, one time, didn't constitute a romantic attachment. For some reason, the posturing didn't help improve my spirits and the walk home with Vanessa was mostly in silence on both our parts, as if she'd clued into my mood.

A few minutes after arriving back home, Vanessa announced that she was going to bed.

I poured myself a glass of wine and was sitting in the large chair in the livingroom when Vanessa appeared in the doorway. She said, "If I have no luck at Charlie's house tomorrow, I may wait near his garage door at the hotel and follow him if he leaves in his car."

The latter plan explained the grilling I'd gotten earlier about Charlie's life at the hotel. "Well, be careful."

"Ah," she laughed, "I will. … And I was thinking … the people who dine at the restaurant with Charlie might also be worth looking into. And maybe even following. Is there any chance that you could get me their names?"

"Honestly Vanessa, I haven't a clue about how I'd do that. Nothing is written down. I mean, Charlie doesn't give us names. His messages just tell us how many guests he'll be hosting and at what time."

"Understood."

"But, now that I think about it, the next time he's entertaining I could ask around among the staff and try to make it sound like casual interest. Maybe someone will know a name or two. Actually, I did that without thinking yesterday, and Lumina knew the guy at dinner was Brian Hemmings. I'll keep asking her."

"Brilliant." Looking earnestly at me, she said, "Can you promise me something?"

"Of course."

"Whatever happens, anything, no matter what it is or how strange it seems, if you don't see me for a period of time, promise me that you won't go to the police and tell them what I'm up to."

"What are you thinking?" I said, feeling alarmed. "What might happen?"

"Don't worry. I may find Sam and take her somewhere to hide. I may be watching some house overnight. I may need to hide somewhere else. If I disappear I don't want the police looking for me. If I have Sam I don't want anyone to know she's with me. I'd rather they figure I've gone home. And I don't want you to assume the worst, but to trust me."

I agreed with Vanessa's request but her comment that she might need to go into hiding somewhere else reminded me once again that she was engaged on a potentially dangerous quest. She'd been attacked once already for what she was up to and that wasn't something to treat lightly.

Stage Direction for the theatrical version of *Playing With Shadows*.

To be projected onto the stage screen.

Wednesday.

I slept till 10:00 AM, had something to eat, and took the opportunity, in Vanessa's absence, to check out the usual online sources in the hope of finding some work. I then touched base with my agent.

With that out of the way I stared at the bedroom wall, bathed in a sense of futility, while trying to come up with some ideas for The Other Theatre's next production. A complete blank. There were too many things going on in my private life.

I told myself that a plot is what your characters do over the time frame of the story, so with no luck coming up with a plot or play subject, I asked myself who would make an interesting character. Still nothing.

My ruminations reminded me that I hadn't checked my email in a couple of days. I opened it and found that Dag had sent around a subject proposal.

He'd written a long email suggesting a subject idea that was 'local' and 'personal'. He was from the northern part of the province, and enthusiastically urged that our new play focus on the closure of the Northern Pulp mill near Pictou. The mill had been shuttered by the provincial government a few years back because its dumping of treated effluent into nearby lagoons had apparently created a toxic mess. It had been labelled 'environmental racism' due to its effect on the land and livelihood of the Pictou Landing First Nation. The mill's proposal, to instead pipe its waste into the Northumberland Strait, would have destroyed the local fisheries.

Dag wrote: "We could present the varying views of the owners of the mill, the Native band members, the local residents, fishers, politicians."

The proposal was well-received. Dag's idea to cover five viewpoints matched the size of the group. The only concern expressed in the responses from the group, was that none of us was a Native.

I weighed into the discussion, writing that the person responsible for that fifth of the production could—instead of acting—present audio and video documents that they'd recorded of the Natives who'd been affected.

I hit 'send' and signed off my email.

I got the word from Lumina, when I started my shift, that Charlie Lawrence would be dining in his penthouse suite with a single guest.

At the usual time, I took the food cart containing dinner and wheeled it into Charlie's elevator, riding it up to his suite.

Once inside, I began setting the table, and was just about finished when I heard loud voices from behind the French doors that led to the rest of the suite.

It was impossible to make out most of the words being exchanged beyond the doors, try as I might, but it was clearly an argument.

I heard a woman's voice say something about 'the boss' and then about 'needing money for the plan'. And there was a sing-song refrain that sounded like 'lies, lies'.

Charlie's responses weren't discernible. But as the French doors swung open, I heard him say, in a paternalistic tone of voice, "Trust me Windy-May, I'll phone him. We can talk then or set something up. Everything about the plan is settled. I don't see what he needs more money for."

The polar bite in the air was palpable as Charlie and his companion entered the room.

I tried to keep my head down—even more than usual—but I happened to glance at the young woman and saw that she was flushed and angry.

Charlie was subdued. He said little, except to affirm the wine of the day would be fine, and "Thank you" when I left the room.

On my second trip to Charlie's dining suite—to bring the food—neither of the diners were present. And not a drop of wine appeared to have been consumed.

Charlie had signalled that the dinner was concluded by leaving a $100 bill beside his plate: my usual tip.

As I stacked the dishes back onto the dinner cart, I wondered if I'd seen the woman for the last time.

I now knew who she was though.

I recognized the name, Windy-May. I'd heard it before and I didn't need to rack my brains to remember where.

Several years earlier I'd been living in an apartment, on my own, in a building overlooking a downtown Halifax park.

One hot summer Saturday afternoon I was sitting at my desk, my front window open because of a lack of air-conditioning, when I was jolted by the sound of the gunshot that killed Tanya Thomas, an anti-racism activist.

She'd been standing at the foot of a statue, in the centre of the park, speaking to a group of people about ridding the city of place names that celebrated racists.

I watched the aftermath unfold out front.

The murder was an outrage and the entire city had been affected. It was the supreme violation of another human being, stripping her of life, and in the process, undoubtedly destroying her family and friends. I saw her boyfriend on the nightly news crying as he talked about the plans they'd made for a life together.

For me and my neighbours, the shooting had also been a violation of our community and our sense of safety.

The guy who shot Tanya Thomas was a white supremacist named George Attwell. He was said to have acted alone. Apparently some lunatic nutbar radicalized by conspiracy theories online. He believed that the killing would initiate a race war.

In recalling the events of that day, I remembered how pissed off I felt after reading a CBC news story saying that police organizations, at all levels across the country, were conducting surveillance on Black, 2SLGBTQ+, and Native groups, but seldom on the violent far right groups that preyed on them. Tanya Thomas's death might have been prevented were it not for an institutional bias that said people seeking equal rights and protections were out to destroy society while redneck wackjobs were harmless—or even allies.

I hoped that police practices had changed because I kept reading over and over in the news about the growth of conspiracy theories, far right militias, and acts of domestic terrorism. I'd read that neo-Nazis and militia members were infiltrating or walking hand in hand with anti-vax groups, even claiming that vaccines are akin to Nazi doctor Josef Mengele's experiments. And lately, these same sorts of losers had become intent on smashing up Pride parades and attacking the 2SLGBTQ+ community.

A year after the murder of Tanya Thomas, my anger was revived as I followed the daily coverage of the Attwell trial on the nightly TV news. It was during the trial that I'd heard the name Windy-May. Not on the news—because she was a minor, I presume—but from Matilda, a woman I worked with who knew George Attwell's wife Belinda.

Matilda said that Windy-May had gone to Alberta after Belinda deserted the family, a short while before the Thomas murder. I remembered Matilda defending the mother saying, "Belinda has always been an attentive mother. She must have been subject to a lot of abuse from her husband to have gotten to the point where she'd up and run away."

I couldn't recall the name of the place out west where the girl went to live, but her name—Windy-May—remained in my memory bank because it was such a singular one.

Windy-May, it appeared, was now an adult and back living in Halifax.

At the end of my shift at the restaurant, I headed home, again, instead of making the trip to Casey's. It was the third night in a row, and I once more wondered what Stacey might be thinking about my absence. But now with a sense of desperation about the possibilities.

I decided that since I couldn't abandon Vanessa I would follow Lumina's advice and try to convince her to come to Casey's with me. I picked up my pace.

As I approached my house I noted that the lights were on in Mrs. Tate's flat. Extremely late by her standards.

She wasn't at her usual post at the front window, however. Nor did she magically appear as I climbed the inside stairs to the apartment.

The knot in my stomach—the one that always manifested itself as I ran the gauntlet between the front door of the house and my flat—quickly eased.

I put my key in the lock and turned it. The door wasn't locked. Surprised, I gingerly pushed it open. There were no lights on, and the apartment was silent.

I flicked on the hall light and tentatively walked to Vanessa's room after seeing that her door was wide open.

I turned on the room's overhead light. All her stuff appeared to be there—but she wasn't.

From there I went to the front window of the apartment. The street below was empty. I craned my neck to look left. Then right. No Vanessa walking up the sidewalk on her way back from the store.

Continuing to watch—growing increasingly anxious—I eventually told myself to remain calm. Vanessa had just gone out for a walk. She'd been going stir-crazy.

Turning from the window, I told myself to follow my usual routines. That would still my anxiety which I told myself was an over-reaction.

So I turned on a lamp, poured myself a glass of wine, and sat in the recliner. My unwinding after work ritual.

It wasn't an overly successful plan as the fact of Vanessa's absence kept sneaking back to the forefront of my thoughts.

I recalled her exact words the evening before: "I may find Sam and take her somewhere to hide. I may be watching some house overnight. I may need to hide somewhere else. If I disappear I don't want you to assume the worst, but to trust me."

I'd been forewarned that Vanessa might not be home tonight and she'd told me not to worry, so trust that everything is fine, I told myself.

Maybe—and my spirits soared at the possibility—she'd found Sam at Charlie's place and was keeping her in a secret location.

I let the calming effect of that possibility sweep over me.

I picked up a book and tried to read. Damnably though, my thoughts found their way back to Vanessa's absence.

I once more went to the front window and my eyes swept the side of the street, I swore to myself. There was my mother's car. And it was in a different spot from where I'd left it, meaning that Vanessa had gone out in it but returned here at some point.

Once again it seemed that, in all likelihood, she'd just gone for a walk or to the store. The apartment door had been unlocked when I got home after all. Proof that she expected to be back sometime soon.

At any moment, I told myself, I would hear the street door open and I would feel embarrassed for my neurotic worrying.

With that in mind I sat back down in the easy chair and picked up my book. But instead of reading, I found myself listening. I froze, and listened intently, with every click or squeak from the house, and from Mrs. Tate moving about in her apartment. Of all the evenings to suddenly turn into a night owl she'd chosen this one.

None of them signalled Vanessa arriving.

I put on some music, turned low so as not to stir the wrath of my landlady, leaned back in my chair, and closed my eyes.

Bad idea.

I recalled the two goons that were on the lookout for Vanessa. Had they found her? Her plan had been to watch

Charlie's house. She may have been spotted there. A thought that had been lingering came to mind. At one point, when Vanessa was talking about the attack on her at the soiree, she'd said that Charlie employed goons who would 'kill' people. She'd quickly amended the statement, but had it been a slip of the tongue or was murder the goon's intention?

The hell with it, I thought. It was impossible to sit.

I returned to the front window to survey the street below. Ghost town quiet. Not a soul passing by. Not even a vehicle.

Should I ask Mrs. Tate if she'd seen or heard anything unusual?

Just then I heard the old lady's floorboards crunching once again. I knew Mrs. Tate—or at least I thought I did. If anything untoward had happened during the day she'd have called the police. Or at the very least she'd have ambushed me with a complaint the moment I stepped foot through the front door of the house.

Should I call the police? I'd promised Vanessa that I wouldn't, but what if my inaction was putting her in danger? What if she was being held by the goons and every minute mattered?

But, I told myself, if I did call the cops, what would or could they do? With no sign of a break-in, they might see my concern as an over-reaction. And it possibly was.

I had only one option. To wait.

Thursday. One week since I'd gotten the idea of sneaking into Charlie's party.

I woke up. Abruptly. Like I'd been given an electric shock; going from deep, deathly sleep to wide awake in a split second. I felt disoriented.

Sunlight was engulfing me so I closed my eyes to withstand the assault of cheery normality.

I re-opened them to see that I was still fully dressed, and laying on top of the bed covers. I questioned myself about when I'd gone to my room but got no answer.

When my memory of the previous evening intruded, about returning home to find Vanessa absent, I opened my eyes with determination. I glanced at the clock: 1:14 PM!

I jumped up and checked Vanessa's room. She still wasn't back.

I returned to my bedroom to double check the time on my alarm clock. I hadn't misread it. The stress of the night before —and maybe the days before that—had obviously exhausted me.

A short while later I was sitting at the kitchen table nursing a bland cup of instant black coffee. From downstairs came the muted sound of voices from Mrs. Tate's radio, or maybe her TV.

I revisited my reasoning during the early morning and reassured myself that I was making the right decision in saying nothing to the police about Vanessa's disappearance. I quelled any conflicting thoughts, without complete success, that I was making the right call. Vanessa was not in trouble and didn't need help. Maybe she'd found Sam and, at this very moment, the two of them were winging their way back to New Zealand.

I busied myself getting ready for work.

I got the surprising news as soon as I set foot in the restaurant's kitchen: Charlie Lawrence was entertaining in his room but he'd be serving himself.

It was the way things had been handled in the past, before I'd been designated as exclusive server.

I'd thought that Charlie had decided to keep me on as his private server, but now it was looking like I was wrong. I wondered if this new arrangement was to be permanent and if it had something to do with what I'd witnessed the evening before.

Far from being upset about the blow to my earnings—as I would have been if I'd lost my special gig a few days earlier —I was delighted. With my new change in status, I might be able to stay in my job at the hotel, at least for now. since I would have no contact with Charlie. The tips would be smaller but I could squeak by.

My work situation was definitely looking up.

In the midst of the dinner rush, I was occupied with a table of diners when I spotted Charlie leaving the kitchen. He was pushing the dinner cart used to stage dinners in his suite.

He entered his private elevator and turned. As the door was sliding shut, Charlie caught sight of me. He smiled, and even gave me a quick wave.

Perhaps, I thought, depressed at the possibility, that maybe Charlie serving his own dinner wasn't reflective of a new status for me. Maybe it was just a one off.

After rushing home from work, I spotted Mrs. Tate, her nose to the front window, inspecting everything on the street. I nodded in her direction. She nodded back and didn't confront me when I went through the front door of the house.

What miracle was this? For the second night in a row she was up well past her usual bedtime.

On entering my apartment, I immediately went to Vanessa's room and confirmed that nothing had changed.

It would be another long night of trying not to worry and of concocting scenarios to explain Vanessa's absence. Maybe, I thought, I should head for the pub, my usual haunt on a Thursday night. In the company of others I might manage to escape my own concerns. And I would get to visit with Stacey.

But I didn't. I made it a whole block, walking in the direction of Casey's, before I began to worry that, amidst the loud din, I might not hear my phone if Vanessa called. She didn't have a phone of her own but everyone else did, so it would be easy enough to borrow one.

I turned around and headed back to the apartment, knowing that I might spend half the night perched at the front window, like Mrs. Tate, watching the street below.

And that would be followed by another restless attempt at sleep.

I think that the most distressing thought I had was: what if I never heard from Vanessa again?

As I walked, I became distracted, once again, by the thought that it was strange that Vanessa didn't own a cellphone. This time, it occurred to me that she also didn't have email. She relied on snail mail. I'd seen a letter from her sister. And I remembered her mentioning that the laptop she used for her research had been borrowed from a friend—so she didn't have internet access either. It was like she wanted to live in an earlier era.

I made a note to self that I had to stop worrying about Vanessa and get on with my life.

By the morning I had backed off on that resolution.

Friday.

Before I left home in my mother's car, I searched Vanessa's bedroom for a photo of her daughter. How else would I recognize Sam if I saw her? There were no framed photographs set out on the desk, dresser, or bedside table, so I went through Vanessa's luggage.

I felt guilty about it, even knowing that my motives weren't exploitative or selfish. It felt like I was Sophie Calle, the artist who Isadora had told our theatre group about, who'd gotten a job as a chambermaid in a hotel to photograph people's private items in their absence.

I didn't come across a single photo of any sort. Surprising and odd. I'd assumed that Vanessa would have at least one photo of her daughter to show to other people when asking them if they'd seen her.

Stupid of me, I thought. Of course Vanessa would have the photos on the camera she'd have with her.

Disappointed at the results of my search, and relieved that I hadn't been caught at it, I put on my shoes then launched myself down the stairs to the front door.

During my sleepless hours, earlier that morning, it had occurred to me that while I'd promised Vanessa I wouldn't go to the police if she failed to return, it didn't mean that I was committed to doing nothing. I could look for her and Sam.

I stopped at Canadian Tire before heading out of town.

The drive to the Lawrence house, reinforced my suspicion that Addison was fully aware that Charlie entertained his mistresses in his hotel suite. While his home was in the countryside, it was no more than thirty minutes from the hotel. There was no logistical reason that Charlie couldn't have commuted.

I didn't have to search for his house, having found it online.

The place was situated on a paved country road, at the top of a rise, overlooking the ocean. It was set maybe thirty metres back from the road.

I slowed my mother's car as I drove past, and rubber necked. There were gates at the head of a brick driveway. They were open but the angle of the drive, plus the positioning of a large number of trees, made it impossible to see the entrance to the house.

The problem that presented itself—that I'd known was coming—was: how could I watch the place without me or my parked car being seen and/or raising suspicions? The extent of my planning had been to decide to make a plan once I'd had a chance to look around.

After passing the Lawrence house, I drove for two minutes or so and then stopped on the side of the road. I hadn't seen anywhere to park where the car wouldn't draw attention.

I made a u-turn and drove past the house again, going in the opposite direction, and continued on for another two minutes. It was the same disappointing story in that direction.

On consideration, my best option for parking somewhere that wouldn't draw attention, seemed to be the north-south gravel road that ended almost directly opposite Charlie's house. And that's where I headed.

I turned up the gravel road and drove a couple of hundred metres along before pulling over and parking. There was nothing but bush on either side of me. Perfect. This was Nova Scotia. A vehicle parked on the side of an empty road that cut through the bush wasn't something to be remarked on. Someone taking a leak. Maybe car trouble. Even a hunter or angler. No one would think anything of it.

The bush was damp and there was only a lacklustre wind. Heavy clouds muscled each other overheard. I'd known it would be a bugfest sitting in the bush all morning so I'd bought the most expensive mosquito repellent in stock at Canadian Tire, assured that it would ward off attacks from anything and everything.

As I walked in the direction of Charlie's I liberally doused myself with the vile smelling spray.

When I got back to the paved road, I scooted across it and

into the bush beside Charlie's house.

It was a slow, stumbling trek to get to a spot that was parallel with the building.

I then edged my way forwards, keeping low until reaching what appeared to be the optimal spot for my lookout. It was far enough from the house that I could watch the driveway and entrance, as well as part of the front lawn on the ocean side.

I crouched down in a slight hollow, behind a fallen tree that was mostly rotten. I saw three cars parked by the front entrance. And one of them was a police cruiser.

It was a surprising sight, but not an alarming one. There were many innocent possibilities for why the cruiser might be there.

I noted some coloured Muskoka chairs on the ocean-side lawn but there didn't appear to be any steps leading down to the water.

The house was modernist by design, lacking any ornamentation at all. A plain box with expansive windows overlooking the sea and the forest. The windows took up almost the entire front of the house and even wrapped around the corner nearest me. It made me think of Charlie's private dining room within the hotel restaurant. The guy seemed to have a desire to be watched. I repositioned myself, closer to the ocean-side front of the house so that I had a good view of the interior.

I made out three figures standing and talking in what appeared to be the dining room: a woman that I was certain was Addison, another woman, and a uniformed police officer.

I saw no kids.

I removed the muted phone from my pocket and took a photo of the scene to be examined later. If nothing came of my visit I might at least be able to advance Vanessa's scheme to identify Charlie's friends.

My working plan was that I would stay in my current position for a couple of hours—more or less. If I saw nothing I would move my camp to the other side of the house where I could take up a similar view. It didn't seem that there were any better places to watch from.

By 1:00 PM I'd shifted position and the police cruiser was long gone. Five other cars had come and gone, remaining for various lengths of time. They'd all been photographed. I recognized the faces of two of the visiting men from having served them at The Seaman's Grill but I couldn't attach names to the faces.

One of the visiting cars included two girls.

I had a better opportunity to study them than the adults since they hung about the front yard. But neither was near Sam's age.

With my nerves on high alert, I'd even watched while the girls poked around in the bush immediately in front of my hiding spot at one point.

By mid-afternoon, I'd seen enough to feel satisfied that Sam wasn't being held at the house and Vanessa wasn't watching. It was time to head home and get ready for work.

As soon as I rounded the final street corner on my walk to The Seaman's Grill, I knew that something was seriously wrong. There were no less than six police cruisers, along with other police and emergency vehicles, parked in front of the hotel.

There were several small groups of people milling about on the sidewalk across the street.

I went around to the back of the building, to the staff entrance that I normally used. A short cop, obviously addicted to weightlifting, stood at the entrance. He puffed himself up and told me that I couldn't go inside.

"But I work here," I said.

"Just a sec." The officer's feet remained planted on the pavement as he twisted his torso to look behind him. "Doug, Doug," he called, to a second policeman inside the building. "I have another employee here."

Officer Doug, who was studying a clipboard, raised his head to take in the new arrival then walked over. "Could I get your name?"

"Peter Russell."

Doug scanned the top sheet of paper, his eyes going up and down a list, deathly slow. He licked his finger then flipped the page over. He studied a new list and eventually said, "Okay, yes, here you are. You worked last night." He looked at me, his eyes making the statement into a question.

"Yes, in the restaurant."

"Well, we'll need to get your statement. Come with me."

I followed Officer Doug through the door and caught up with him as we walked down the hallway toward the elevators. My pulse quickened with anxiety, and my voice cracked when I whispered, "What's going on?"

"You'll be briefed when you make your statement, sir."

I obediently followed the officer into the restaurant which was obviously now closed to the public. Some of my fellow employees were sitting at the tables normally occupied by diners. They all looked up momentarily.

"Have a seat please, sir." Officer Doug waved his hand to indicate the entire room was available. "They'll call your name when they're ready to interview you."

I took a tentative step forward and looked about. The upscale dining room was decidedly downscale at that moment. Only the bright overhead lights used by the cleaners were on. None of the customary tablecloths were out and chairs were propped upside down on most of the tables. Kitchen staff, servers, and front desk staff sat around five or six of the fifteen tables.

Between some upturned chair legs, I spotted Lumina sitting by herself. She nodded in my direction then aggressively waved me over.

I crossed the room and took the chair beside her. Again, my voice dropped to a whisper when I leaned forward and asked, "What's going on?"

"It's Charlie," Lumina replied, gripping my arm. "He's dead. They found him a couple of hours ago. Someone apparently killed him last night. I don't know how or if they have a suspect."

"Jesus!"

"So they want to speak to everyone who worked last night's shift, apparently anywhere in the hotel. I'm guessing they'll want to know if any of us saw anyone suspicious or … you know, that sort of thing."

We lapsed into a surreal silence as we struggled to adjust to this new, bizarre reality.

My gaze went from one to another of my fellow employees. A couple of them were dabbing their eyes but I heard no crying. The rest seemed to be in the same sort of shocked disbelief as Lumina and I. They spoke in quiet whispers although I did overhear someone, whose voice punctured the sombre quiet, say, "I know that Charlie had his faults but he didn't do anything bad enough to deserve this."

Employees continued to be led in. They invariably looked about desperately, until spotting a friend, then rushed over to an oasis of familiarity.

Jimmy Ross, the hotel receiver, marched across the

restaurant when he saw me. Jimmy spent most of his workday at the back of the building where he manned the loading docks and the storeroom. He was the staff's unofficial greeter and always had a story or three to tell if he nabbed someone arriving while he was outside smoking.

I was one of his regular targets, since I would stop and talk, although our conversations mostly consisted of Jimmy's monologues about sports pools, hunting, and his impending or recent vacations.

"Helluva thing eh?" Jimmy said as he sat down, shaking his head.

Lumina and I agreed.

"I found him you know," Jimmy added,

I imagined that my and Lumina's eyes must have widened because Jimmy quickly added, "No kidding. We got a call from Charlie's wife right after I got in this morning, and Shelley at the front desk asked me to check on him. Seems Charlie hadn't answered any of his wife's messages since yesterday morning. I've got the manager's keys so I went up to Charlie's suite. He was lying face down on the carpet in the middle of the livingroom. The back of his head was smashed in."

"My god!" said Lumina. "Do the cops have any idea who did it?"

"Nope," Jimmy grunted economically.

I had never before seen Jimmy at a loss for words before; an indication of the severity of the shock he'd experienced.

In spite of myself, I couldn't help imagining Charlie laying on the floor of his suite, the back of his head crimson from matted blood. I inhaled slowly and looked about to rid myself of the image.

Jimmy eventually broke the silence when he leaned forward, looked left and right, and said softly, "I did see something strange though. I worked a little later than usual last night, receiving supplies cus of the convention starting next week. I nipped out for a butt around 4:30, or maybe a bit later, and there was a woman hanging around by Charlie's garage door."

"A woman?" said Lumina. "Who?"

"I don't know. She had blonde hair … or light red … hard to tell. She wore a long sort of coat with big pockets. Youngish I guess, but I didn't get much of a look at her. She was standing on the other side of the dock, beside Charlie's personal garage door, and she had her back to me. I said hello to her, as a question like, and she just said 'hello' back. As soon as she says that she walks away up the lane."

"Did you tell the cops about her?" Lumina asked.

"No. I haven't been interviewed yet but I will."

"Would you recognize her?" I asked.

"No. She turned her face a bit when she spoke to me but she sort of had her hand over the side of her face, like she was shading her eyes, but it made it so I couldn't see her face. That's why I wondered if you'd seen her and knew who she was. Oh, and she had an accent. Australian or New Zealand or something like that."

The wind was knocked from me, but I immediately attempted to mask my reaction to Jimmy's comments by adopting a stoic demeanour.

"Aren't there video cameras back there?" asked Lumina.

"There's one, above the receiving door. Depends on which direction the woman came up the alley whether she's on it," said Jimmy.

"And there's one above Charlie's garage door too. I've seen it."

"But it's just for show. Charlie keeps it—I mean kept it— shut off … cus of the young babes he'd take up to his place. I think he might have been scared that something would get recorded and be used to blackmail him—but that's just my theory. … I wonder if this woman was one of his babes. Maybe she was trying to hide her face, standing the way she was. I think that when I stepped out of the door she turned her back to me." He looked in my direction. "Do you think that's suspicious?"

I fumbled for words, trying to find my voice. I'd been thinking that the murder explained the presence of the police car outside Charlie's house that morning. I said, as matter-of-factly as I could, "Might be suspicious, I guess. Maybe not."

"Yeah, that's what I was thinking too. She could have just

been waiting for someone."

"Do you think the woman might have slipped into Charlie's garage when the door was open?" Lumina asked.

"I don't know," said Jimmy. "I don't know if the door was opened last night or not."

I remembered that I'd seen Charlie pushing his food cart into the elevator during the previous night's dinner service. Had there been two entrées on the cart? Since Charlie would pick up and drop off the women he brought to his suite, he might have exited and entered the garage a couple of times during the course of the evening—so two opportunities for someone to slip through an open garage door.

A police officer walked into the room and called for attention. He explained the process for interviews. They would call a name and that person would be taken to the hotel office. There would only be a few basic questions, 'a sorta debrief' was the way he phrased it.

The first name he called was Jimmy's.

The smell of coffee alerted me to the fact that Celine—one of my fellow servers—was circulating with a tray full of cups of coffee. When she stopped at my table I declined. My stomach was already in knots. If Celine had been distributing stiff shots of liquor I might have grabbed one or two.

Lumina got up and began to help with the coffee. I should have too but it didn't occur to me at that moment. I had too many other thoughts competing for attention.

I wondered what was happening in Charlie's suite. Would it be the way it always was on TV, with forensics people swarming all over in paper booties, masks, and coveralls to protect evidence? Examining every inch of the place. What would they find? Could they tell who had been there besides Charlie?

And I wondered about Vanessa. Had she been the woman that Jimmy saw behind the hotel? She'd told me that if she found nothing at Charlie's house that she might wait by the garage door and follow him. But … The murder was Thursday night. Vanessa had last been at my apartment on Wednesday and so far as I knew my mother's car hadn't been touched since then. Unless Vanessa had rented a car, she wouldn't have been here to follow Charlie.

I forced himself to turn off any thoughts along these lines. I had to stay in a public mode, in the moment, and leave reflection for later. I decided to say nothing in my police interview that would incriminate Vanessa. I needed time to think.

As Lumina was sitting back down, across from me, she said, resuming the tone of conspiratorial whisper, "Celine said that the police are going up and down the alley looking for Charlie's car. For some reason they think it should be in the basement but it's not."

I put the news aside. It would have to wait for me to stir it into the mix of things to consider. "Maybe Addison told them about it."

"Yes, Addison. ... This will be hard on her, of course. I feel sorry for her, but then I have for a long time."

"Yes, well, I don't know what she knew about Charlie's women, like you said ..."

"It's not just the affairs. I gathered that Charlie was stringing her along about something else."

"What was that?"

"I was walking behind Charlie and Brian Hemmings the other night, on their way to the dining room, and I overheard Charlie saying that he was surprised how well she was doing babysitting a kid that wasn't even her own."

"She was babysitting a kid? Who? Did he mention who the kid was?"

"Not that I heard. His family, maybe. ... But it turns out—no great surprise—that Charlie was a lying prick. Hemmings asked him if he was going to give her the role she wanted, for babysitting, and Charlie just laughed and said no, that she couldn't act or sing so she'd just embarrass both herself and him."

Stage Direction for the theatrical version of *Playing With Shadows*.

To be projected onto the stage screen.

Stage Direction for the theatrical version of *Playing With Shadows*.

To be played out behind the stage screen as the employees continue to sit in front of it.

Interviewer

You're a server here at the hotel as I understand it.

Peter Russell

Yes. Dinner service only. I'm an actor otherwise.

Interviewer

Right. I was told that you were the sole waiter who served Mr. Lawrence in his suite when he ate here during the week.

Peter Russell

During the week, that's right. But I didn't serve him last night.

Interviewer

Yes, I'm aware of that. Did Mr, Lawrence explain why the exception?

Peter Russell

No.

Interviewer

Do you know who his guest was last night?

Peter Russell

No.

Interviewer

In your experience, serving dinner in his suite, how many different guests would you say he had?

Peter Russell

It was always the same guest.

Interviewer

Male of female?

Peter Russell

A woman.

Interviewer

A mistress?

Peter Russell

I don't know the nature of their relationship since Mr. Lawrence never confided in me.

Interviewer

I see. Do you know this woman's name?

Peter Russell

No.

Interviewer

So you never heard Mr. Lawrence call her by name?

Peter Russell

No.

Interviewer

Can you describe her, this woman?

126

Peter Russell

Young. Blonde hair. White skin.

Interviewer

How young is young?

Peter Russell

Maybe nineteen, twenty at a guess.

Interviewer

Would you be able to identify her if you saw her again?

Peter Russell

Maybe, maybe not. I was paid to be discrete which I took to mean that I shouldn't pay attention to the woman. Charlie watched me closely, plus he was the boss, so I focused my attention on him.

Interviewer

Did you see Mr. Lawrence last night? And if so, when?

Peter Russell

I saw him getting into his private elevator by himself, pushing a food cart from the kitchen. It would have been close to 7:30 because dinner service was in full swing.

Interviewer

Was anyone with him?

Peter Russell

No.

Interviewer

Did you see him bring the cart back to the kitchen?

Peter Russell

No.

Interviewer

And you … your shift ends when?

Peter Russell

At 11:00.

Interviewer

And what time did you leave last night?

Peter Russell

About 11:15.

Interviewer

And you exited the building through which
door?

Peter Russell

The staff entrance at the back.

Interviewer

And what time did you arrive at work for
your shift?

Peter Russell

Around 4:10.

Interviewer

And do you use the staff entrance when you
arrive?

Peter Russell

Yes.

Interviewer

Did you see anyone when you came in? A
fair-haired woman in a long coat perhaps?

Peter Russell

No.

Interviewer

If there was such a person there yesterday afternoon, do you have any idea who she might have been?

Peter Russell

No.

Interviewer

You have a key to the penthouse and the private elevator?

Peter Russell

Yes.

Interviewer

And there's only two sets of keys, apart from Mr. Lawrence's?

Peter Russell

So far as I know.

Interviewer

Can you access the penthouse from the stairs?

Peter Russell

Yes. There's a locked door at the head of the stairs on the top guest floor. It leads to a flight of stairs that go up one floor.

Interviewer

Do you have a key for that door?

Peter Russell

Yes.

Interviewer

Do you know of anyone who would want to
kill Mr Lawrence?

Peter Russell

No.

Interviewer

Is there anything that I haven't asked about
that you think might be relevant?

Peter Russell

No.

The restaurant was closed for the day, so I walked home, oblivious to my surroundings having become absorbed with the question of whether Vanessa had been the woman who Jimmy had spotted behind the hotel.

The description of the woman matched Vanessa's appearance—if she was wearing Ellis's wig. On the other hand, it was a limited description. How tall was the woman? How old? Did she have an Australian or New Zealand accent? They aren't the same. And was she wearing a hat?

If it was Vanessa, had she seen something or someone that forced her into hiding as a result of having been there? The murderer perhaps?

The possible scenario was both alarming and reassuring. But it left even more questions. Why, for example, would she have gone into hiding when she was already hiding at my apartment?

I recalled our late night walk when we'd run into Stacey. Vanessa had asked for details about the hotel, the location of Charlie's suite, and how it was accessed. I'd willingly answered her questions, and provided information about the private garage entrance leading to a private elevator. I'd even told Vanessa about the fact that the camera in the area of the garage door was disabled.

Had she lain in wait outside the garage door waiting for Charlie to leave so she could slip inside when the door was open? She may have had a plan to sneak into Charlie's suite, to look for information about Sam's whereabouts.

If Charlie had left to drive his dinner date home he might not have been away for a long period of time, so, if Vanessa had successfully snuck into the hotel and made it to Charlie's suite, she may have been surprised in the act and ...

I couldn't keep following that line of reasoning. Vanessa wouldn't do something violent, I was sure. I dismissed the idea entirely.

But my certainty wavered. I remembered Vanessa telling

me that she might disappear and asking me, if she did, not to speak to the police about her. The implication was ominous.

Had she planned to murder Charlie?

It was nonsense of course, and I chastised myself for the thought. Vanessa had no reason to want to kill Charlie Lawrence. She, of all people, would want him alive since he might lead her to her missing daughter. There was no way she would have gone to the hotel for the purpose of killing him. It didn't rule out the possibility that something unplanned had occurred …

Again, I shut off a line of reasoning. This time with the thought that when I next saw Vanessa I would tell her that I now knew that Addison was the person looking after Sam— somewhere. Vanessa would be thrilled by the news. I didn't have a location for where Sam would be but Addison could be followed easy enough.

By the time I arrived home, I had reaffirmed my immediate impulse to say nothing to the police about Vanessa. Let them figure things out.

I had no doubt that I would mull things over, involuntarily, and maybe even question my conviction, but I had zero evidence that she was involved with Charlie's death.

And she wasn't the only person whose name I'd withheld from the police. I wondered about my impulsive decision to say nothing of Windy-May.

I considered the matter and concluded that it must have been because I felt sorry for her. For starters, she'd grown up with George Attwell as a father and had likely been subject to his vile bilge. She may have been bullied by other kids growing up, or made an outcast by her association with a murderer. And then there was her involvement with Charlie. She couldn't have been long out of her teens—if she was even that—meaning that she would have been ripe for exploitation by a wealthy older man.

I resolved that, as was the case with Vanessa, I would continue to say nothing to the police about Windy-May since I had no idea of whether she was involved in Charlie's murder—even knowing that she'd been angry and arguing with Charlie the previous night.

I was resolute but downcast about my decisions to keep so many things secret. Downcast because I knew something about the danger of secrets. The fallout from keeping them had been a theme of our play, *The Secret*. I knew that the repercussions of silence could be manifold and even dangerous.

But it was the path I'd decided on. The matter was settled. I would slip back into the comfort of the shadows.

So there it was. I was a free man. Time to leave all this stuff behind.

At 8:00 PM I lay down on my bed. It wasn't dark, but I was exhausted from the day and wanted to close my eyes for a few minutes.

Unexpectedly, I fell asleep and when I woke up it was going on for 2:00 AM.

I was angry at myself because the last thing I remembered thinking, before I nodded, off was that I would head for Casey's later and hopefully connect with Stacey. I could reclaim my own life, which had been on pause. and escape the frightening and unfamiliar circumstances I was caught up in. But exhaustion from stress had temporarily decided otherwise.

But sleep wouldn't come now that I wanted it to.

In spite of my resolution to get on with my life, I found myself worrying about Vanessa. Was she okay—and what now was to come with Sam? I didn't do indifference well.

Saturday. A lost day for the most part since I spent it hanging around my apartment.

I distracted myself with the emails going back and forth between The Other Theatre members as they batted around story ideas for our next production.

Murder was on everyone's mind.

Both Isadora and George's suggestions involved mass shootings.

George wanted to focus on the slaughter of twenty-two people by a lone gunman in 2020. He suggested we focus on a small group of people hiding from the killer.

Isadora meanwhile, wished to delve into a murder-suicide committed by a veteran suffering from PTSD. She had a well-thought out proposal for how we could cover the event but it was immediately clear that none of us were likely to accept her idea. Our last play had focused on an act of violence committed by a man with PTSD as a result of war.

Both of these suggestions were important stories where voices needed to be heard—and I reflected that this would have also have been the case if we did something involving people's experiences with Hurricane Fiona—but the feeling was that we should continue to generate story ideas. *The Secret* had been a personal story and the general consensus was that we should first explore whether any of us had story ideas about something that affected us directly.

"What do you have Peter?" Isadora asked me in an email. As with all emails, everyone in the group had been copied.

I cursed when I read the thing. It caught me off guard. I still had nothing.

But I began to type anyway, taking my cue from the others. "I've also been thinking about a murder. The murder of Tanya Tucker."

I went on to relate the story of sitting near my window, overlooking a park, and hearing a gunshot. I wrote about the victim and seeing her family on the nightly news. I wrote what I knew about George Attwell. Mentioned that he had a daughter, so there was a wide circle of victims. Including the community. And I outlined some of the issues that were at work in the killing of Tanya Thomas: racism, the rise of the far right, police surveillance failure. These were all more significant now than ever.

To my surprise, after sending out my email, my colleagues responded positively. The suggestion had clearly generated some enthusiasm.

People began to bat around ideas about how to approach the subject. Many felt that using audio or video recordings of all involved parties would be the most interesting approach. Each member could interview one individual.

I'd thrown out the play suggestion just to seem to be contributing but it seemed, on quick reflection, that it wasn't a bad idea … until what came next.

Lumina wrote: "Peter, you said that you have a friend who knows the family and that it was her who told you about George Attwell's daughter. Maybe your friend knows where the daughter is living. She must be an adult by now. Since the child was one of Attwell's innocent victims, I wonder if you'd be willing to contact her for an interview?"

I was quick to reply: "I would, but I can't speak to the woman who told me about her because she's passed away. I think it might be very difficult to track the daughter down since the clan will likely try to shield her."

Lumina responded: "Yes, I'm sure that could be the case, but we don't know. Would you try?"

I muttered a curse, but agreed. This was one of the last things in the world that I wanted to do. Windy-May had connections to Charlie Lawrence and I wanted nothing to do with his world or his murder. I regretted that I'd put the idea forth to focus on the Thomas murder.

When Dag proposed that the play focus on my story it occurred to me that this might be my out. Neither me, nor anyone in the group, had been personally involved in what happened.

"No, no," I wrote, "I don't want this to be seen as *my* story.

It involved two families—those of the killer and the victim—as well as everyone else who was there; like the police and the public. I'm about the fifty-seventh most involved person in this story. A casual witness of the aftermath."

In spite of my response, Lumina wrote. "I agree with Dag that, so far, this is the best suggestion we've had. Frankly, due to the murder of Charlie Lawrence I haven't been able to focus on coming up with play ideas. Can we let this sit for a few days and pick up the dialogue next week?"

Everyone was agreeable.

I shook my head. Why hadn't I thought to say that earlier?

Dag wrote: "Lumina/Peter. Charlie's murder affects both of you! And you have contact with a bunch of people who knew him. While you're considering good play premises, please consider whether the murder itself might be one of them."

I closed my email.

Leaning back in my chair I looked at the ceiling. Which play would I least like to do; one about the murder of Tanya Thomas or one focused on the murder of Charlie Lawrence?

We wanted a personal story and, sad to admit, my life at the moment was bound up with what had happened to Charlie Lawrence. My current predicament could be the subject of the play. But that wasn't going to happen!

What about doing something that was completely fictional, I thought? I'd seen lots of movies and TV shows. I know how they go. There's a murder. Then a body. Then the cops and the coroner show up. Then some cop asks the coroner for a guess at the time and the cause of death, and the coroner puts the cop in his or her place: 'You'll have to wait till I've examined the body'. The cops then post photos of everyone involved in the case on a white board and they begin to interview. They'll hit a dead end until the coroner finds something startling. Something in the victim's throat, or that they were terminally ill, or pregnant. It will lead to the solution to the crime in the end. How hard could it be to write something like that?

In my final email I'd agreed to meet up with the gang for dinner.

It was a bad idea. All anyone wanted to talk about was the murder of Charlie Lawrence.

Because of the conversation, I ended up, lost in my own thoughts on the subject. Then something occurred to me.

If the blonde haired woman hanging about Charlie's garage door had snuck in and killed him, and it wasn't Vanessa, then might it have been Charlie's wife, Addison. She had blonde hair and, as an actress, could likely fake an accent. She'd been excluded from his life at the hotel where he entertained his mistresses. She may have watched Charlie drive away from the hotel with Windy-May. Would it be a surprise if Addison felt humiliated? Or if she'd had enough and decided to punish Charlie?

No! No! No! Be it resolved. If it came down to one of the two murders to focus on for our next production, it wouldn't be Charlie's if I had anything to say about the matter.

137

The name of the police detective who showed up was Ryder.

When I opened my apartment door I looked down and saw him. already standing at the foot of the stairs, speaking to Mrs. Tate.

She looked up when she heard my door and called out, "The police are here to see you." I took her self-satisfied tone to mean something like, 'I knew you were up to no good'.

Ryder pulled an ID from the pocket of his sports jacket and flashed it in my direction.

"C'mon up," I said.

The detective was a large, lumbering man who was wheezing by the time he reached the second floor. He paused just inside the apartment door to catch his breath.

He looked about and his gaze fell on the full-size framed movie poster, hanging an arm's length from his face. It was for an early Hitchcock film named *Murder!*.

Ryder studied the poster for some time before shuffling into the livingroom, at my invitation, and lowering himself onto the couch.

I took a spot on the recliner, facing him.

After some niceties about appreciating my help, and indicating that he only had a few questions, Ryder got down to it and asked abruptly, "Is there a woman staying here named Vanessa Sutherland?"

I managed to maintain my composure despite the rush of adrenaline. How did the police knew she'd been here?

"No," I said.

"But you know her?"

"We've met."

"How did you meet?"

"At Charlie Lawrence's annual soiree."

"Have you seen Vanessa since then?"

"I have." No point denying it. The fact that Ryder was here meant that Vanessa had somehow been tracked to my apartment.

"Where was that?"

"She came here. She forgot her purse at the Lawrence party and she stopped by to see if I'd picked it up."

"And had you?"

"Yes. I got her address from a letter in the purse and even tried to return it to her place but she wasn't home. So I kept the purse and she came here."

"And did Ms. Sutherland stay here after that."

"She did … for a day or two." What else was I to say? Despite my promise to Vanessa that I wouldn't tell the cops anything, which I intended to honour, I had to say something that was believable.

"And why was that?"

"She felt that it was too dangerous to go home."

"Why?"

"Her ex was stalking her, she said."

Ryder stared at me momentarily. Maybe assessing me. Maybe determining what to say next. "Do you know where Ms. Sutherland is now?"

"No. I thought she went home. She could be still hiding I guess."

"From her ex?"

"Presumably."

"And did she tell you the name of her ex?"

"No." My first outright lie.

"Did you tell Ms. Sutherland at the soiree that you were employed by Charlie Lawrence?"

"No." Did I? I couldn't remember.

"How about when she was staying here?"

"I mentioned it, yeah."

"Uh huh. And did she ask you about your job and if you ever overheard anything your boss talked about?"

"I told her what my job was. The question of whether I overheard anything of his private business dealings never came up … and I never hear anything by the way."

"So Mr. Lawrence and his guests were mute when you

were around?" Ryder sounded incredulous.

"Exactly."

In spite of my response, Ryder began to ask the same questions, just clothed in different wording. Had I ever overheard anything about Charlie's business or personal affairs? Had Vanessa asked whether I did? Had I passed anything on to her? A particularly inane question given that my answers to the previous questions were negative.

"And what about information flow the other way?" Ryder said. "Did Ms. Sutherland ever reveal anything to you that she'd discovered about Mr. Lawrence?"

"Discovered? No." I was becoming exasperated. Why was I being questioned about Vanessa? "Do you think Vanessa is connected to Charlie's murder?" I said.

Ryder didn't respond. "Did Ms. Sutherland ever speak about her own work?"

"No. I think she said she was a teacher when she was married but that's the extent of it."

I observed Ryder's eyebrows rise.

The detective paused in thought before continuing. "Did Ms. Sutherland ever ply you for information about Mr. Lawrence's personal affairs?"

"No. Haven't I answered that? Same answer. We never talked about the guy in any way, shape or form. Nothing." How had this clown gotten through cop school? Annoyed, I let my composure get away from me. And that's when I should have known it was time to shut up. "She did say that she was frustrated with the police who were making no effort to help her find her daughter who was kidnapped by her ex husband!"

Ryder was seemingly unaffected by my attack on his force. Instead, he said, "Thank you," and wrestled himself to his feet.

I followed suit.

Once erect, Ryder pulled his sports jacket around his massive waist. Looking me in the eye, he said, "Mr. Russell, would it surprise you to know that Ms. Sutherland was never a teacher, was never married, and has no children?"

"No, I don't know her. I only know what I was told."

"I understand the urge to keep things to ourselves with the idea that we're protecting people. If that's the case here it's misguided. Lying to the police is serious business. People make themselves accessories to crimes. So, in light of what you now know about Ms. Sutherland, is there any part of what you've just said that you'd like to retract or alter?"

I looked blankly back at Ryder. "No. I'm not protecting her and I have no idea where she is."

"Okay, fine. Will you let me know if she contacts you?"

"I will," I lied.

He said that he was fresh out of business cards, so I needed to jot down his phone number. After I'd done so, Ryder said, "Oh, and did you ever take a photograph of Ms. Sutherland?"

"No."

As soon as the detective left the house, I went to the front window and watched him drive away.

I then began to pace. The hell with what Mrs. Tate thought. I could care less if she objected.

I was angry with myself. Why, I thought, had I taken to scolding the cop about the police not helping Vanessa? By doing so, I'd said a lot of things that I should have kept quiet about. Things that were implicitly included in my promise to Vanessa to keep mum about. I should have told Ryder nothing other than that Vanessa was briefly here, that she was gone, and I knew nothing about her.

Had I been baited by the cop? Probably. It was likely why he kept on asking me the same questions over and over. Getting me to lose my composure.

By shooting my mouth off I'd revealed that Vanessa had fed me a bunch of lies. That would only reinforce whatever suspicions he had about her that she was up to no good.

I paced.

Another question came to mind: If Vanessa wasn't who she represented herself to be then who the hell was she?

I went to my laptop. Logged online. I searched, 'Vanessa Sutherland' and 'New Zealand'.

Several articles came up, not only from New Zealand but also from America. It seemed that Vanessa had been living in the States for the last few years.

I read the lead paragraph of the top four articles that came up in my search. Vanessa was variously described as a photographer, videographer, and conceptual artist.

I settled in and began to read the fifth article.

Vanessa had apparently begun as a documentary photographer whose efforts were 'political'. Her first show attacked urban development for its blindness to places where, despite the shabby surroundings, people lived in communities full of life. These were plowed over. In Before and After photos, Vanessa captured images of new, sterile spaces that catered to corporate and well-heeled clients, and contrasted them with images of the bleak places where the former residents now lived because their communities were gone.

I learned that she continued to work in this same documentary (apparently a characterization that she objected to) vein.

The article said that many galleries had begun to reject Vanessa's work as not being 'art' but journalism, so she'd taken to displaying it in store windows—where her videos, with subtitles, would run on a continuous loop for passersby —in union halls, and even in bars.

Vanessa didn't make a living from her work because she didn't sell it, the article said.

I moved on to other stories about her, including an article on a gallery website introducing a new show. The piece was entitled: *Living In The Shadows.*

Stage Direction for the theatrical version of *Playing With Shadows*.

To be read in a voice over and accompanied by this still of Vanessa, taken from *Living In The Shadows*, projected onto the stage screen.

Vanessa Sutherland is a photographer who refuses to travel in the light, choosing instead to remain invisible—as much as possible anyway.
With this is mind, she has chosen not to have any credit cards, cellphones, or

internet access (so no social media accounts). And there are no photographs of her face anywhere, even from childhood (facilitated by having been home-schooled by nervous parents who refused to allow photos of their daughter to be taken).

She is one of a growing group of young photographers whose work is focused on exposing the wealthy and influential who ordinarily stand in the shadows. Exposing their social lives, their use of off-shore shell companies and other means to avoid taxes, and the charity work they support in order to advance their own interests under the guise of benevolence.

Sutherland began as a documentary photographer. When she came to feel that her efforts were having little effect, she made a complete 360, influenced by the work of Hans Haacke.

In her current exhibition, *Shadows*, she returns to the subject of slumlords. She focuses on those who live in their buildings. Following the same format as her recent shows, she pairs two sets of photos along with plaques that describe what we are looking at. But this time, her shows include much more.

In one case, we see images of a slumlord living the high life, hanging beside images of the impoverished residents of one of his rotten buildings. And accompanying written text provides a lengthy list of the renovation work that the landlord has been ordered to undertake. Other photographs reveal that none of the work has been done.

To take her photos of the wealthy, Sutherland has became a stalker of sorts, tracking people who either avoid the spotlight or keep their private lives out of the press.

She was influenced by a work of Daniel Mayrit, where pictures of his wealthy, shadowy subjects were made to look like CCTV images because that was how poor people often appear in the media. A look that screams 'this is a criminal'.

Sutherland's black and white, photo realist images of the wealthy (using the same technique employed for her documentary photos) levels the playing field.

By not presenting the wealthy as glamorous, in slick and colourful images, they appear to be dull, unexceptional, and self-absorbed.

Is it hypocritical that she makes herself invisible while exposing others? Is it hypocritical that someone who has never been the subject of a photograph spends so much time surreptitiously photographing and video recording people, their homes, and their lives?

When I spoke to her over the phone, Sutherland answered 'no' to these questions.

'I see no contradiction. The seeming hypocrisy is an implicit critique of a society where being surveilled is ubiquitous; where huge amounts of data are compiled about each of us to sell us things, to spy on us and uncover our associates, and to keep us in line. Meanwhile, the activities of the wealthy and powerful go largely undetected. Both are reflections of life today. I simply want to flip these positions. I want to take the role usually reserved for those in power—like those who use social media sites to delve into their employees'

personal lives—and to put the owners under the microscope.

My shows are also meant to chastise the failures of mainstream media by making use of public information that the press ignores. All of the information that I've gleaned about my wealthy subjects is readily available online, with only the slightest amount of research, but it is generally ignored.'

Her lack of a public presence, she told me, is also a means of self-protection from those she exposes.

I got up from my desk and headed for the sidewalk with no destination in mind. I needed to sort out my thoughts after what I'd just read.

To begin with, it suggested why Vanessa had been at Charlie Lawrence's soiree. The party was a social event that attracted the wealthy and influential. In all likelihood, she'd gone there for the purpose of photographing someone—or a group of people—that she intended to expose.

If that was true, it would explain why the security people had treated her with hostility. Vanessa was supposed to be some sort of master of invisibility—living in the shadows— but for the security people to know her she must have been poking around during her weeks in Canada.

I remembered one of Ryder's questions. He'd asked if Vanessa had revealed anything she'd 'discovered' about Charlie. It told me that it must have been Charlie she'd been at the party investigating. The fact that she'd grilled me about Charlie confirmed my view.

But why, I wondered, had Vanessa spun such an elaborate story for my benefit? A story about a kidnapped daughter and the rest of it. It was especially weird since the lies came after I'd told her she could crash at my place for a bit. She hadn't needed to tell me anything.

I should have seen through the lies, I told myself. I'd observed how dispassionately Vanessa had been when telling me about her child being kidnapped. She hadn't demonstrated the sort of emotions one would expect to see from a parent in that situation.

Having gleaned more information about Vanessa than I knew previously should have answered some of my questions, but instead, I was now more in the dark rather than less.

It was quite possible, I was now ready to concede, that Vanessa had broken into Charlie's suite looking for something or other. It would be out of character given what I'd just read—that she relied on public information for her work—but she obviously could have gone to Charlie's suite to search it. And what then? Had he come home? Maybe the cops had found evidence of her presence at the suite and that was the reason why they were so fixated on her.

I was suddenly afraid—for myself. The effect of my helping Vanessa and then believing her lies had been to drag me into the middle of a murder investigation. And I felt sick at the thought.

As I'd been trudging along, I'd been oblivious to my surroundings. But I began to look about and saw people sitting on their porches to take in the sunshine. Others were working in their yards. It was a week since I'd gone looking for Vanessa to return her purse.

I still wasn't ready to presume that she was a murderer but I weighed the option of telling the police everything I knew— for my own self-protection and to get out of any future involvement in the matter.

Then a frustrating possibility occurred to me. If I went to the police and changed my story I'd be admitting that I lied to them. Would that be grounds for them to charge me with having hindered an investigation?

And it could also be much worse. An admission of lying might even lead them to think that I'd been involved in the murder and that I was now trying to throw the blame Vanessa's way. After all, I had access to Charlie's suite and Jimmy hadn't mentioned anything to suggest it had been broken into.

It was enough. A week of life spent worrying about and protecting a liar. I doubled down on my resolve to put this episode in my life behind me and to think no more about it.

I turned the key in the lock of my apartment door. Surprisingly it was unlocked. Evidence, I thought, of just how distracted I'd been when I left to go walkabout.

But I halted abruptly with the door half open. There was someone inside. I could hear what appeared to be dishes being washed.

I stood still, listening, my hand on the doorknob.

Deciding to take a bold approach, I went to the kitchen door.

Someone was indeed doing the dishes. Standing at the sink with her back to me. Her hands in the soapy water, dealing with the three days of dirty dishes that I'd been too distracted to care about, letting them pile up haphazardly on the counter beside the sink.

"Hello," I said neutrally.

Vanessa started, then spun about and smiled as if there'd been nothing to change our relationship since she'd last been here. "Hello," she said.

"I wondered if I'd ever see you again."

Vanessa appeared to be genuinely perplexed. "I told you that I might disappear for a few days." Apparently noticing the look on my face, she added, "Do you want me to leave?"

"You told me you *might* be going away but I didn't know why you did … so I was worried."

"I'm sorry. I should have left a note."

"The police were here," I said flatly.

"And what did they say?"

"They were looking for you. I guess your landlady told them where you were."

Vanessa arched her eyebrows in disbelief. "I told Mrs. Page I was staying with a friend, but I didn't mention your name. So the police didn't get their information that I was staying here from her. My guess is that the security people from Charlie's party figured out who the person who helped me was and then told the police."

"Where have you been?" I asked.

"When I got back here on Tuesday afternoon, Mrs. Tate stopped me on the stairs. She said that a car had pulled up with two men in it but neither got out. They just watched the house ..."

"The goons ..."

"I think so."

"Wait ... and Mrs. Tate told you?"

"Yes. She said that after I left here that the men did too. Apparently, some time later in the day, another car parked outside. And the driver of that car also watched the house. He was still here when I got back ... anyway, to make a long story short, I told her about my situation and she invited me to stay with her till I felt safe to come back upstairs. That's where I've been."

"With Mrs. Tate?"

"She's a nice lady. Lonely maybe, and definitely nosy, but kind. The only reason I didn't move downstairs straight away on Tuesday was so I could give you a heads up that I'd be away when you got home on Wednesday. That's why I asked you not to call the cops when you didn't see me."

"So you told her what was going on but not me ..." I cut myself off. I'd been about to complain about being kept in the dark about the goons. Like I was looking for repentance or to make Vanessa feel guilty. "But you're here. Aren't you worried that the goons will come looking for you?"

"No. I planned to stay downstairs but I thought that since they gave my name to the cops that they'll back off. I'm not their problem any more."

"It does make sense that it was the goons who figured out where you were. They saw me at your place. I would have also been on CCTV and Charlie could have given them a name to go with the face ... but it's odd that the cops care about you. The goons obviously told them a story because it seems like you're a person of interest in Charlie Lawrence's murder."

"Really?" Vanessa's composed tone remained, even with the revelation. "I heard a bit about the murder. Did the cop say why they think I'm involved?"

"He didn't say that's what he thought. I only inferred it from his questions. It sounded like he thought you were investigating Charlie and maybe stumbled onto something."

"And I what, murdered him for it? What would that be?"

"He didn't say. I don't think he knew of anything. He was trying to get that from me. … Oh, and there's something else. A woman was spotted outside the garage door behind the hotel awhile before Charlie was killed in his suite. She had blonde hair, a long coat, hid her face, and had a New Zealand or Australian accent."

"That wasn't me!" Vanessa drew her head back in surprise as if there was something in my face that would explain what I'd said. "But you thought it was …"

"I wondered, but I knew you weren't connected to what happened with Charlie. It was the accent thing. Otherwise, it could have been anyone. Maybe even Addison, Charlie's wife."

"And you think she was spying on him? Maybe looking to confront him about his affairs?"

"Just a theory."

Vanessa didn't reply. She just stood there staring at me until eventually saying. "For the record, I wasn't looking into Charlie's business affairs—not at all."

It was a few minutes later. … We'd taken seats in the kitchen when I said, "I betrayed your confidence that I wouldn't speak to the cops."

"It doesn't sound like you had any choice."

"No, that's not true. I got pissed off at the guy's continual prodding. He kept asking whether I, or you, had uncovered any dirt on Charlie. Over and over. I ended up giving him shit for going on about that and not looking for Sam."

"Ah. And he told you that I don't have a daughter."

"Yeah. Obviously I looked you up online after his visit … just a second. I want to check on the apartment windows and make sure that they're closed."

During our conversation the kitchen had grown dim and a heavy rain had to begun to fall, pounding a tattoo on the roof.

I hesitated when I got to the front window in order to gather my thoughts. Things were moving too fast. I wanted to be able to control the flow of the conversation with Vanessa when it resumed so that my questions about what she was up to could finally be answered.

The house across the road was just a blurry outline—so fierce was the rain—yet I could still make out the stream of water gushing from the bottom of the drain pipe at the corner of the house. It looked like someone had opened a fire hydrant.

On the street immediately beneath me, two people were running for cover like bombs were dropping, shielding their heads with their hands.

When I returned to the kitchen, I found that Vanessa had finished washing the dishes in my absence, and they were now drying in the dish rack.

She was, once again, standing, but this time with her back to the counter.

I stopped in the doorway and leaned against the frame, facing her. "It's really coming down out there. Anyway, as I was saying, the detective wanted to know if you'd told me anything about stuff Charlie was up to or if I knew of anything and had told you."

"And what did you tell him?"

"Nothing about that. And I didn't tell him you were asking me about Charlie's suite and the hotel …"

"And now you're wondering if I went to Charlie's suite. I admit, I was curious and at the time I was wondering if it would be possible to check out his apartment on a day when he wasn't there, but I didn't."

"But why even consider if? If there's no missing child, what would you be looking for?"

Vanessa didn't immediately respond. Eventually she took a deep breath and said, "I should start from the beginning. … Can we sit?"

I agreed and we went into the living room.

For the second time that day, I found myself sitting on the recliner, opposite someone on the sofa.

"I like your poster. How appropriate." Vanessa nodded to a framed movie poster, for the film *Singin' In The Rain*, hanging on the end wall.

"Yes," I agreed. But I wasn't interested in pleasantries. "I'd like to know why you lied to me about you having a daughter," I said.

"I'm sorry. I didn't trust you since you worked for Charlie. You could have only invited me to stay so you could watch me. I thought that you'd be more likely to take my side and break with Charlie if I gained your sympathy—I mean if you were pals."

"Take your side about what?"

"I'm honestly only here in Canada to look for a little girl and I thought that Charlie would know where she was. Everything I told you about spying on Senior's family and the others was true. I watched their houses and Sam wasn't there."

"But she's not your daughter?"

"No. She's the daughter of Ev Collins and his wife Katie, who was my best friend. Katie died from breast cancer last year. After her death, Sam—and that is her real name by the way—went to live with her New Zealand grandparents. I was being honest when I told you that Ev had little interest in Sam. Katie's parents wanted to adopt Sam, and Ev was happy with that. He thought it would be for the best—and it would have been. No one knows exactly what happened but we think that Ev's father got to him and convinced him to bring Sam to Canada. One day, like I told you, Ev took Sam out for a visit and never brought her back. He sent Katie's parents a text saying that he'd decided to keep her and that was that." Vanessa paused and again inhaled deeply, like the memories evoked by the act of explaining were physically taxing. "We only found out that Sam was in Canada after Ev's sister sent an email to Sam's grandparents to say she was here."

"Did they—Katie's parents, I mean—try to get custody?"

"Legally? Sort of. They saw a lawyer but he said that their chances were pretty much nil if Ev wanted to keep her. Unless they could prove he was unfit and posed a danger to Sam."

"Even though the little girl's a New Zealand citizen?"

"Even then. Ev's the father and there's no case to be made against him. He was pretty disinterested in Sam but all he needed to say was that things had changed. Katie's parents have been really worried about Sam though because they know nothing about what's happening with her, so I decided to come here for a visit and check on her."

"And you haven't found her …"

"No, and I was being honest when I told you I was only at the party to try and locate Ev. I wanted to track him down and follow him to wherever Sam is. He's not a bad guy actually, just under the thumb of his old man. And that guy's a piece of work. He flatly refused to let me see Sam and told me to go home. His goons threatened me, like I said. I just want to see Sam, for my own satisfaction, and that of her grandparents, to know that she's okay. I promised them I would. They want her to know that she wasn't rejected by Katie's family. Sam may be being fed a bunch of lies by Senior if he's in control; and that's a concern. According to what Ev told Katie, he lived a sheltered life growing up with Senior, and it was a daily indoctrination into Senior's political views, racism, and sexism—like I told you."

"So the goons did beat you up on Senior's orders."

"I think so."

"Why is he so adamant about keeping Sam from you?"

"He didn't say. He just said that Sam was his business and none of mine. Maybe he thinks if I find her I'll kidnap her and take her back to New Zealand. Or maybe he thinks I'll poke my nose into his business—I mean, given the fact that it's what I do."

"You think she's being kept somewhere just to keep her from you?"

"No. I doubt I matter so much. My guess is that she's

boarding with a family who can look after her. Senior's on his own. I can't see him looking after her. Same with Ev. That little girl has no one."

"But will you kidnap her if you find her?"

"Well the thought has crossed my mind, but no, I wouldn't. Ev's the father and everything is up to him. Plus, I'm not saying that Sam is being abused or anything. I just want to check on her; under supervision even."

"And they won't even let you do that."

"No, and that's what's getting me worried. … Sam's under the influence of her grandfather, and I know Katie wouldn't have wanted that. Sam will be indoctrinated into his extreme views."

"Charming. So you're still having to be a detective of sorts. It sounds like something you're good at."

"It is similar; looking for guys who stay out of the public eye. Difference is that here I've been trying to discover who Senior's friends are. In New Zealand and America I at least knew the names of the people I was stalking."

I said, "Is it true you've never had your picture taken?"

"No. That's not possible. There's CCTV everywhere. Plus I have a driver's license and a passport. On the other hand I do try to remain in the shadows. I don't have a library card, sign petitions, go to political rallies because the cops film them and … well, you get the idea."

"I noticed your expression when I first mentioned that I worked for Charlie Lawrence. You obviously hate him. Why?"

"I went to see him, like I told you. I knew that he was a friend of Senior's so figured that Sam could be with his family or he at least might know where she's staying. And he was awful to me. I told you about the way he was. … I didn't look into his business affairs, like I said, but I did look him up online trying to find out if he had a wife and kids. And I saw something about his past. Seems he's a wonderful guy, just like his buddy Senior."

"He came from the States they say."

"He did. He's from the south and his name came up in the case of the murder of a liberal politician by a far right militia.

He was part of the group that the cops thought was responsible, although he wasn't charged. He came to Canada right after that."

"I wonder if that has anything to do with his murder."

"I don't know and I don't have a guess. As I said, my only interest is in finding Sam."

"And you watched his place."

"Twice this week alone. I watched all Wednesday and Addison was there by herself. She went out a couple of times but she left and arrived alone ..."

"I'm not doubting that. I watched the house most of Friday and there was no little girl there. But I'm not convinced that Charlie wasn't involved in keeping Sam. My co-worker Lumina told me that she overheard Charlie one night, earlier this week, talking to Brian Hemmings. They were talking about someone who was babysitting some kid and Charlie said that he was surprised what a good job she was doing."

"And it was Addison he was talking about?"

"Er ... I don't know, to tell you the truth. But apparently Charlie said that he'd promised the babysitter a juicy part in one of his plays if she babysat but he wasn't going to do that because she was such a terrible actress."

"And Addison is the world's worst actress."

"Exactly. Draw your own conclusion."

An hour had passed since my conversation with Vanessa in the living room. In the intervening time, she'd been in her room with the door closed while I sat in my room, behind my laptop, trying to locate Windy-May. Why? I was confronting the inevitable; that The Other Theatre might be taking up the subject of the murder her father had committed and I wanted to at least be able to say that I had tried to locate her.

When Vanessa reemerged, she stopped at my open door. "You look like you're deep in thought," she said.

"I suppose. I was wondering about a possible connection between Charlie's murder and Sam's disappearance."

"You think there was one?"

"Possibly. First off, you mentioned that Senior holds far right views and indoctrinated his children into them. And Charlie was part of a far right group ..."

"If I can interrupt—sorry—I don't think that Senior holds the same views as the far right. Others may use that term to describe his politics but I don't. I think there's a distinction between his sort of conservatism and violent militias. From what I remember Ev telling us, Senior and his friends seem to be those conservative leaning people who have drifted to extreme positions. They champion autocratic leaders around the world and want to undermine democracy here. It's hypocritical given their phony freedom fighter rhetoric. They don't want to pay taxes and hate a democratic system where the majority of the population can insist they pay their share, and can create laws to impede their ability to exploit the environment and other people."

"I've not heard about this ..."

"No, because they choose to operate in the shadows. They do things like fund biased university chairs and organizations —like those that deny climate change. In the U.S. you also have groups funded by untraceable dark money. Their latest aim is to try to assert States' control to strip the federal government's power."

"But they don't do that in Canada."

"I don't know. … The lines between the two groups on the fringes of the right do blur. The wealthy in the States own big media networks and fund politicians. They spew their rhetoric and hate, and then people act on it, and commit hate crimes. You've probably heard about all the conspiracy theories that exist online, but I think the most damaging hate speech comes from so-called 'respectable' right wing media and politicians that foment hate to get themselves into power. They operate in the open. They say they are doing this and that cruel thing to protect our children—even though there's no threat. The other is always cast as a threat that the hero politician must save the populace from. Their audience lives in an echo chamber of media and social media propaganda saying the same things, so they come to accept a false reality. Their bigotry—based on ignorance—feels to them like it's real and rational. It's Plato's cave. People with power who cast innocent people as threats, sparking hate, have blood on their hands."

While Vanessa was speaking, it came to mind that there were parallels between the current vilification of immigrants and people in the trans community to what happened on the east coast in the nineteenth century where poor Irish Protestants turned against Irish Catholic immigrants, duped into thinking that they were a problem. Scapegoating and scare-mongering. "Oh. Okay … well, point taken. I was maybe going too far because I was surprised when you mentioned that Charlie had past connections to the far right … because there is something else that supports the idea of far right involvement in his death."

"What?"

"Charlie's mistress. I heard her name the other night. Wednesday, I think it was. She and Charlie were having a fight and he called her Windy-May."

"Okay …"

"Yeah, an odd name. And a distinctive one. I think she's the daughter of George Attwell. He's a far right murderer who assassinated a young Black woman at a rally several years back. She was speaking out against places and things around

Halifax being named after racists."

"And you're thinking she killed Charlie?"

"No. Well, it's a possibility but I'm thinking that the connection suggests that Charlie was still involved with those violent groups. The woman—Windy-May is her name—was a kid living out west at the time of the murder but she came back here and she hooked up with Charlie. I wonder how that happened. The fact that she's the daughter of a far right killer, and that Charlie once had far right connections, makes me wonder if they're both part of that community here."

Vanessa paused, considering my theory, before answering. "I can see why you think that they have social connections. It makes sense. But to conclude that they're part of a far right group ..." she seemed to wince like she was in pain, "... I don't know about that."

"But there's more. The last time I encountered Windy-May and Charlie was during their dinner in Charlie's suite, the night before his murder. She was yelling at him. Something about someone she referred to as 'the boss' needing more money for some plan or project."

"Any idea of what this plan or project was?"

"No. But Charlie obviously did, He told Windy-May that he'd set up a meeting with someone he referred to as 'the boss'. I think it's possible that he and Windy-May were caught up in something together with this boss. ... What if the boss was the murderer?"

"I'm not questioning your judgment, but being involved in some business activity with someone doesn't in itself suggest it's something nefarious. ... So, the boss? Any ideas about who he is? If he's not a business associate maybe he's a pimp."

"Not likely," I shrugged. "What plan or project would a pimp be involved in with Charlie?"

"Yes, I see, and it's unlikely that a pimp would have killed Charlie because he wanted more money."

"I wouldn't think so. Anyway, leaving all that aside, Charlie knew where Sam was and knew the woman looking after her ... I think that we can say that with confidence."

"Well, having spoken to him, I agree that he likely knew

where Sam was being kept. But I would say that we can only be certain that he knew the woman looking after Sam if she was the little girl he was talking about."

"True. But how many little girls could Charlie have a part in arranging babysitting for?"

"You're the one who knows him …"

"Exactly. And babysitting wasn't his thing. Windy-May was close to Charlie so she could know something about Sam. I think you should put her on your list of people to investigate."

"Okay. So do you know where she lives?"

"Not a clue. Sorry. But I'm looking for her. The theatre company I'm part of is likely taking on the story of George Attwell's murder of Tanya Thomas as the basis for its next play. And I've been assigned the task of tracking down Windy-May and talking to her. Not something I'm thrilled about but if I can find her I can try to get some information."

"Now who's playing detective. You're on the track of a killer? Ah …" Vanessa was clearly dubious.

"No, no, not at all. I should talk to Windy-May about her father for our play. But, like I was saying, since Windy-May and Charlie were likely part of a group of friends then it's possible she knows something about Sam. And if we find out who killed Charlie … well … it gets the cops off your tail."

Vanessa didn't respond, which I took to mean that she was dubious about the idea.

Look," she said, "the sun's out."

I hadn't noticed until then but the torrential rain had stopped.

Sunday.

"So tell me about this new theatre project of yours," Vanessa said.

We were together in the kitchen eating breakfast.

I brought her up to date on what had happened so far with our next play, and the uncertainty of whether the murder of Tanya Thomas would end up being our subject. "Before the possibility came up, we decided that we would take on something that was personal to at least one of us. Because I witnessed the aftermath of the murder they thought that it qualified as a personal story. It makes me feel uncomfortable because the group seems to think that I'm a part of the event. And that's not true. I just glimpsed a bit of it. Sure, I was affected, but I wasn't involved in any way."

"Why does it have to be personal? Aren't the issues raised important?"

"They are, but we don't want to speak for others. If the Tanya Thomas murder isn't the subject of the play, Dag suggested we do something about the murder of Charlie Lawrence."

"So more of a personal connection there. Maybe you could tell your story of the hunt for Charlie's killer. I'll grant you exclusive access to my story."

"But I'm not hunting. I'd rather just distance myself from anything to do with Charlie's murder. I'm only interested in looking for Sam and pursuing the Tanya Thomas story."

"Too bad, because I have a theory about the blonde-haired woman with the New Zealand accent skulking behind the hotel."

"So not Addison?"

"No. Like I told you, I watched her place twice this week. What I didn't mention was that the second time was Thursday. I took Mrs. Tate's car. It was the same afternoon the mystery woman was at the hotel."

"And Addison was at home?"

"Yes, and she never left the house."

"And could you see inside? I could only make out the inside, when I was there, because it was so overcast, almost dark and the lights were on in the house ..."

"I was there till midnight. When it was totally dark, I even walked right up to the window and looked inside, my face was centimetres from the glass."

"Ah."

"Anyway, since the blonde wasn't me and it wasn't Addison, I was thinking ... well you'll probably think me a conspiracy theorist but I'm wondering if maybe the intent was to set me up."

"Who would do that?"

"Well ..." a concerned look spread across Vanessa's face, "maybe a killer who wanted to throw the police off their trail."

"But how would whoever did that know anything about you?"

"Charlie knew about Sam, and about me. It tells me that Senior shared information with his buddies. That the murderer knew enough about me to try and set me up suggests they're part of the same group. Doesn't it?"

"So you're saying Senior is connected to Charlie's murder? Like he's 'the boss'?"

"No, no, no, I have no evidence of that. I'm only saying that Senior must be part of this hypothetical circle of friends that Windy-May and Charlie are part of ... and that so is whoever killed him ... because the person knows about me. Jesus. I just thought of the implications of that. It means that Sam might be staying with someone within that group."

"Do you have any proof, I mean other than what the sister said, that Sam is with a family friend and not Ev?"

"No."

I fell silent and Vanessa followed suit. She got up and went to the washroom.

On her return, Vanessa resumed sitting and said, "By the way, out of curiosity, did you tell the police detective about Windy-May?"

"No."

"That is interesting. Why would you protect her? Are you in love with her?"

"Huh? Now that's a strange question. No, I said nothing because I didn't want to point the cops in her direction because I have no reason to think that she's directly involved in Charlie's murder. I suspect she's part of Charlie's crowd so may know something about Sam but that's all. And I guess I feel sorry for her. I think that, given her lack of experience that she may have been taken advantage of by Charlie."

"Possible, I suppose." Glancing at a decorator clock of Ellis's on the kitchen wall, Vanessa said, "Do you know when Charlie's funeral is?"

"Tomorrow."

"You going?"

"I suppose."

"Maybe Windy-May will be there."

"I think it's unlikely, but it's possible I guess."

"I'm thinking that I should go to the funeral too. I could just watch from the sidelines, if that's possible. I suspect Senior will be there and maybe Ev as well since he used to handle all of Charlie's security. If he is, and we have your mother's car, we could follow him. Or I could."

"Don't forget your camera."

"I never do. Remember you saw me in action at Charlie's party. I take photos and videos of the wealthy at work and play. It's sort of my thing. Or were you thinking of getting some possible documents for your play?"

"Yes … I mean, depending on which play we do … I should compile some documentation connected to Charlie's murder. I'll have my phone with me but I'm not sure if I can take photographs in a discrete way while I'm sitting inside a church. If you're off in the distance, you might be able to."

"Of course. If I get anything worthwhile it'll be all yours."

Stage Direction for the theatrical version of *Playing With Shadows*.

To be read in a voice-over while the image is projected onto the stage screen.

> "The shadow, said celebrated Swiss psychiatrist C.G. Jung, is the unknown 'dark side' of our personality ... Whatever we deem evil, inferior, or unacceptable and deny in ourselves becomes part of the shadow, the counterpoint to what Jung called the persona or conscious ego personality. ... Jung differentiated between the personal shadow and the impersonal or archetypal shadow, which acknowledges transpersonal, pure, or radical evil (symbolized by the Devil and demons), as well as collective evil, exemplified by the horror of the Nazis and the Holocaust. ... Projection of the shadow [onto others] is engaged in not only by individuals, but also by groups, cults, religions, and entire countries ..."
> — Dr. Stephen A. Diamond, in *Psychology Today*

Stage Direction for the theatrical version of *Playing With Shadows*.

To be read in a voice-over while the image is projected onto the stage screen.

> "[Billionaire, Charles] Koch contributed generously to turning those ideas [about stealth] into his personal operational strategy to, as the team saw it, save capitalism from democracy—permanently. … Koch warned, 'The failure to use our superior technology ensures failure.' Translation: the American people would not support their [the radical right] plans [to destroy democracy] so to win they had to work behind the scenes, using a covert strategy instead of open declaration of what they really wanted."
> — Nancy MacLean, *Democracy In Chains*

To my surprise, I learned during our fast food dinner, that Vanessa had spent time that afternoon on her borrowed laptop doing some research on Windy-May. "She seems to be like me," Vanessa said, "in the sense that, like you, I can find no evidence of her existence on the internet, not even from stories about her father. Not surprising, I guess. She wouldn't have gotten into news stories at the time of the murder because of her age, and then later, well … I think that I'd also keep a low profile if my father was a murderer."

"Maybe it's just as well. I don't know what I'll say to her if I do find her."

"I suppose you'd have to try to get her buy-in for doing a play about the murder her father was responsible for but, without knowing what she thinks of her dad it's impossible to know how she'll respond. Maybe you could say that you want to show all sides of the event. That might appeal to her whether she supports her dad or hates him. Once you get her talking you can ask her about other things."

"I suppose … ask if she knows about a little girl Charlie was hiding."

"That could be tricky. It would be like throwing a mystery ingredient into the soup. Who knows what might happen? You have a fifty-fifty chance of a good outcome."

"Yeah. … Oh, I wanted to talk to you about something else. We have a bit of a problem. Lumina sent me a text. She asked if I was going to Charlie's funeral."

Vanessa stared at me, waiting expectantly to hear why this was a problem.

"She doesn't say so but I think she's asking if I'll have my mother's car. A professor of ours died when we were in university. Four of us went to the service together in the car: me, Lumina, and a couple of others. We knew that after the service the plan was to head to the cemetery and that's why I had the car, so we could join in. Lumina doesn't say so—directly—but I think she wants to know if it'll be same for

166

this funeral."

"Do you want to take your mother's car and pick up your friends?"

"No, the important thing is our plans. You don't have much time to find Sam. Once we figure out how it will work with us, I'll reply to Lumina."

"Where's the funeral service?"

"At a large church, downtown."

"Will everyone be driving to the cemetery after?"

"I have no idea. A lot of bodies are cremated and there's no funeral procession. Or so I assume."

"You're right. When we were talking earlier, I was thinking that I'd attend the burial but hang back, in the shadows and watch for Ev. After, I'd follow him when he drove off. The image I had in mind was that we'd be in a huge cemetery but now I have no idea of what I should do."

"Why don't you just confront him?"

"I'd rather just follow him. I don't know how he'd react to me. I think he took Sam at his father's urging so I assume he thinks that father knows best and will follow the old man's instructions to tell me nothing."

We began a back and forth about the funeral, bouncing ideas off each other. A plan began to be formulated.

An hour later I sent a text to Lumina telling her that I was going to the funeral service at the church and that, if there was a procession to the cemetery, I wouldn't be part of it. I said nothing about my mother's car one way or the other so she wouldn't think I lied to her if she spotted me in it.

Monday.

At 7:30 in the morning, Vanessa and I set off for Charlie's funeral together in my mother's Civic.

We arrived at the church an hour before the service was scheduled to commence.

The church had a parking lot but it wasn't a substantial one. For bigger crowds, it relied on a large city parking lot that was around the corner from the church and up the street. Vanessa and I were betting that if Ev attended the funeral that the lot was where he'd park.

Vanessa drove. She found a street parking spot in an ideal location, directly across from the entrance to the civic parking lot. If Ev parked there she'd be able to follow him when he left.

"Good luck," I said, opening the car door.

"I hope you can get back here in time to come with me afterwards," Vanessa replied.

"I'll try. I'll sit as close to the back of the church as I can, so I should be able to escape without anyone taking notice."

I climbed out of the car and walked to the church.

There was a sparse crowd inside so I easily managed to find a spot in the last row of pews, only a few feet from the centre aisle. I held my cellphone in one hand for taking photos or videos, if I found that I could discretely do so.

Shortly after I'd left her alone, Vanessa got out of the car and walked in the direction of the church, but instead of turning left at the corner and going the twenty metres to the steps of the church, she crossed the road, to the three story office building on the corner.

I'd told her about the place. Peggy had worked there one summer, for an insurance company, and I would sometimes meet up with her after work. I always took the stairs and, if I was early, I'd stop at the second floor landing and look out the window. It was a great place to watch the goings on in the street below. "If you stand there you can see both the front of the church to your right and the parking lot straight ahead, up the street directly opposite," I said. "Plus, I think it's close enough that you should be able to make out people's faces when you video them."

Vanessa slipped in among a gaggle of office workers entering the building for their day's work.

She climbed the stairs and stopped at the second floor landing. She told me later that she positioned herself in front of the window overlooking the street while doing her best to tune out the people around her and ignore the possibility that she might be an object of curiosity to some of the people passing behind her.

She said that she felt that I'd been spot on about the window being an ideal place to stand. Not only did it have good sight lines and proximity to the church and the parking lot but there was a chest high ledge in front of the window that she could lean her elbows on to steady her shot whenever she decided to photograph or video record. It also allowed her to position herself so that she was doing those clandestinely; her camera out of sight to the office workers behind her.

The church was beginning to fill up.

I kept my eyes front facing in the hope that Lumina would walk right past when she entered. In the grand scheme of things it didn't matter if she sat behind or beside me but I thought that I'd rather not have to invent an excuse for my exit when the time came.

My positioning allowed me to investigate the goings on in the grand church. I used the time, waiting for the service to commence, by making a conscious effort to study the faces of the people arriving in the vague hope that I might see people who'd been at the restaurant dining with Charlie. These would be people that Vanessa could check out. I hoped that she was getting everyone on video.

New arrivals at the church turned as they made their way along the rows of pews, so I could see them in profile. Small clusters of attendees formed along the aisles, engaged in whispered conversations.

Jeff Weir was there, as was Brian Hemmings. I was pleased that I recognized the nameless faces of several other attendees: I'd also served them in the restaurant as Charlie's guests. I managed to capture their faces in photos.

Some local politicians also went past me. Their presence was unsurprising given that attending the funeral of prominent citizens was an unofficial job requirement.

There was a surprising number of people from the theatre community. One would have been excused for thinking that Charlie Lawrence was a dearly loved figure.

I spotted a few co-workers from the hotel but there was no Lumina. Maybe, I thought, she'd decided to skip it.

Vanessa shot video of people of people approaching and entering the church.

I discovered later that, ever mindful of the fact that she was shooting a video that might be used by my theatre group, she'd maintained a whispered running dialogue the whole time she was shooting.

Her videos of those walking from the parking lot were taken head on, although at a distance, but those of people walking up the steps and into the church—shot from much closer—only captured them from behind.

Vanessa said that she continually lamented being on the opposite side of the street from the church because if she were in the building beside it she'd be recording people's faces from close proximity. In hindsight, she thought that, rather than attending the service, that it would have been a better decision to have me video recording people as well, from the same side of the street as the church.

Thinking about the advantages of the building next door to the church apparently caused Vanessa to study it; not for the first time. But on this occasion something caught her eye. And she trained her camera on it.

A hush fell over the church causing me to turn and look towards the front entrance and the top of the aisle.

Addison, draped in black, was standing just inside the doorway, holding on to the arm of a young man. Her brother, perhaps.

The retinue that soon followed them up the aisle took the empty seats at the front of the church, on one side of the aisle.

Was this like a wedding, I wondered, where the two families sat on opposite sides of the church? If that was the case it meant that Charlie Lawrence's family wasn't in attendance.

171

Stage Direction for the theatrical version of *Playing With Shadows*.

Vanessa Sutherland whispering in the video as it plays, projected onto the stage screen.

Someone's watching and filming from the building beside the church. Let me zoom in to that third floor window.
There. Can you see him? He's not even being particularly discrete; figuring perhaps that no one's going to be looking up.
It's the perfect spot to capture the faces of people attending the funeral.
It must be a cop from one of the police services. It's not the man who I saw go into Peter's flat though.
His presence gives me the creeps. It's something you'd expect to see at a mafia funeral. Is this confirmation that Charlie had some dubious connections: political or business-wise?
Still no sign of Ev. Better get your ass in gear bud, if you're coming.
Let me pan up to the parking lot once again. There's not much action but people are still arriving.
I'm watching each vehicle as it drives in. Trying to see where it parks and who gets out. But it's difficult. You lose sight of whatever car you're tracking cus of all the traffic in the parking lot, moving around, and all the pedestrians.
This would be an ideal time for you to show

up, Ev my boy.

Maybe that's him in the black SUV going through the entrance. He's driving around. I hope he comes to this end of the lot where I can get a good look at him. There's, what, two or three spaces.

C'mon car. Good lad. The door is opening and … and … it is! It's Ev, and now he's hustling his ass to the church.

I'd like to rush outside and talk to him. He was always reasonable in the past but I don't know where his head's at now. Peter said that he saw Ev talking to the guys he calls 'the goons' at the soiree. For all I know, Ev directed them to find me and kill me. He might have even been the one who followed me home; sent the goons to my place. It would spoil everything if I approached him and it alarmed him enough to send Sam somewhere where I can't get at her.

Ev is now in the church so nothing more for me to do here. I wonder if Peter saw the girl he's looking for: Windy-May.

I'll give this a few more minutes and then head for Peter's car to wait for Ev. I think I can find it in the lot and get the license plate number. It may help when I'm following him in case a car just like it gets in the way. I wish I had a tracking device I could plant on it.

This time I drove. It was Vanessa's decision. She was still adjusting to driving on the right side of the road, she reminded me, and figured she might inadvertently drift into on-coming traffic if she became distracted by the task of following another car.

We lost Ev within two blocks. It wasn't my fault. The car in front of us came to an immediate stop when a traffic light turned yellow. Who does that?

"Damn!" I said, then tried to follow Ev's car with my eyes, hoping not to lose contact.

We waited at the light. Agonizing. Ev's car was heading off into the distance.

"He turned right up there, at that next light," Vanessa said, waving in the general direction.

When our signal turned green, I wanted to be off. To do a Lewis Hamilton. But the car ahead just sat. I wanted to lean on the horn but counted down instead. Three … two … The driver ahead puttered off ever so slowly.

I felt faint hope about ever finding Ev when we turned right at the light where he'd turned, but there he was. It was his turn to get caught at a red light.

I stopped my mother's car immediately behind the giant vehicle.

Vanessa slid down in her seat although it was unlikely that Ev would be able to even see the tiny car behind him little own make out Vanessa inside it.

I kept our vehicles almost bumper to bumper after we commenced moving. Vanessa peeked over the dash.

Ev was heading further downtown. "It's like he's going to the Alexander Graham Bell," I said, not that I believed he was, it was just that I would have been making the same turns if I was on my way to work.

Ev turned left onto the street where the hotel was situated and even slowed down in front of it. But he didn't pull into the parking garage or even to the side of the road. Instead, he turned left, towards the building immediately opposite.

He drove down a wide ramp leading to the basement of the new convention centre and stopped in front of a massive garage door at the bottom.

I slowed down and watched, debating whether to follow. I saw Ev's arm swipe a pass at the card reader. It occurred to me that if I went down the ramp, immediately, that I might slip into the building behind Ev before the garage door swung shut. I put on my turn signal but my way was blocked by cars moving in the opposite direction.

Ev drove through the open garage door and it closed behind him. A horn blared and I drove on.

"Did I see the words 'Convention Centre' on that building?" asked Vanessa, now sitting fully upright.

"Yeah, they just built it this year. I wonder what Ev's doing there."

"Well, running building security would be my guess since he's back working for Senior."

I turned right at the first street past the hotel, then right again, swinging the car into the alley that ran behind the hotel. I had no plan, except to get out of the busy flow of traffic and to stop and think. The din and relentlessness of traffic always gets me flustered. Who could think with all the distraction?

I pulled into the space directly in front of the garage door that led down to the basement; to Charlie Lawrence's parking space and elevator.

"What do we do now?" asked Vanessa, surveying her surroundings.

"I don't know. We can't park in front of the convention centre, waiting for Ev to leave, because there's no parking on either side of the street."

"And he could be in there all day."

"We're worse off than we were at the church."

"Maybe I should I go over there and confront him?"

"I thought you didn't want to do that."

"I don't, but we'll lose him if we just sit here."

"Okay. Let me check in with Jimmy, the receiver. I'll tell him that this is my car and to not have it towed. It should be fine—I'd think so anyway—since I don't imagine that anyone's likely to be using this space or needing to get into the basement."

I climbed from the car and walked through the people door on the other side of the loading docks.

I was gone for a couple of minutes and on my return got back into the car and said, "Jimmy's cool with us parking here. I told him you just needed to go to the convention centre for a few minutes. … You still want to?"

"Yes."

"Sorry miss, but you just missed him." The security guard at the front desk said as he hung up the phone. He was a young man, likely a student I thought after noting that the book he put down when we arrived was a copy of *Being and Nothingness*. The identify badge pinned to his navy blue blazer sported the name of Senior's security company.

"Do you think he'll be back soon?" asked Vanessa.

"Since he said he'd meet you here, I'd have to think so, but I don't know."

"Does he have a secretary back at the company offices?"

"You'd have to check with them. Mr. Collins doesn't work here. He's only here because his company is setting up for the convention."

I looked at Vanessa and explained, "There's to be a political convention here later this week. We've been getting ready for it at the restaurant. The hotel is fully booked."

The guard looked expectantly up at Vanessa.

She thanked him, walked away and I followed.

On the sidewalk outside, I said, "So what now?"

"Damn!" Vanessa said. "How frustrating! Well, we know he's going to come back here at some time so this looks to be out best chance of getting hold of him. I have to take the chance and confront him."

"We can watch from the hotel and I can call the security company and see if they can tell me his schedule," I offered.

Vanessa agreed and I got the security company's phone number from the guard.

I struck out on my call however. The woman on the other end said that she had no information about Ev's schedule and, even if she did, she wouldn't be able to give it to me—for security reasons.

The Seaman's Grill was still closed; to allow people to attend Charlie's funeral. It's re-opening was scheduled for the afternoon.

"Not much to look at when there's no table cloths out," I said. We were standing in the main floor hallway, studying the dining room through locked glass doors.

"And there's Charlie's famous glass room within a room, for his play within a play," said Vanessa

"The very one."

I turned to leave and Vanessa followed suit.

We walked down the hall towards the receiving department, and had just passed the two elevators that serviced hotel guests, when I impulsively stopped outside the third elevator. Charlie's personal conveyance. It had a narrower door than the other two and was set apart.

I extracted a set of keys from my pocket, unlocked and opened the elevator door, then stepped inside. I waved my hand, beckoning Vanessa to join me.

She remained standing, nervously glancing up and down the empty hallway before scurrying into the elevator as the door was closing. "Should we be doing this?" she asked.

"Probably not." I pressed the elevator button to take us up to the penthouse.

The door to Charlie's suite wasn't locked.

I tentatively edged it open, peeking inside before hitting the light switch.

I stepped into the unit's foyer and held the door for Vanessa.

She followed me into the suite, tentatively, with baby steps, like something might happen at any moment.

Once we were in the dining room she stopped, her eyes going everywhere, taking in every inch, like a perspective buyer. In a hushed tone she said, "Silk wallpaper. Wow.

Charlie had good taste."

"And money. Enough to hire a first-rate interior designer."

With no agenda, we began to circulate around the room, looking at everything.

I ventured through the French doors that opened into the livingroom of the suite; a room I'd only ever snuck glances at while serving dinner to Charlie and Windy-May.

There was no need to turn on any lights because sunlight poured through the ceiling high windows at the south end. That entire wall was windows, except for a glass door in the middle of it that opened onto an expansive deck.

"Lots and lots of marble," Vanessa said, peeking into the bathroom." She looked in my direction and then to the opposite wall. "You can't see the front of the convention centre from here. Otherwise we could sit up here and watch for Ev to arrive."

I said nothing, distracted with examining the suite; satisfying my long held curiosity.

"As long as we're here, shouldn't we search the place for something that might help us find Sam?" Vanessa said.

"Or maybe Windy-May …"

Signalling our silent agreement, we began, with purpose, to move around the room pulling out drawers. None of them contained papers of any sort, nor was there much of anything else. Even the office, with it's oversized desk, yielded nothing. Clearly the room was an impersonal stage set, meant for entertaining and impressing people rather than a space filled with the remnants of life.

Eventually we gave up the search.

I said. "Should we take some photos and maybe even do a quick video tour?"

"I don't know if you'll be able to use them for your play, since anything we get will be conformation that we broke into Charlie's apartment … but what the hell, why not."

Pulling out my phone, I replied, "Well, technically speaking, we didn't break in. We're just trespassing at a crime scene."

Vanessa and I were installed at a table in front of the fast food restaurant next door to the hotel. A spot where we could watch the front of the new convention centre.

My mother's car was still parked behind the hotel. Vanessa had demurred from her decision to confront Ev, face to face. The new plan was, if we saw Ev going into the convention centre, that I would sprint down the alley and jump into the car. I would then drive to the front of the hotel to rendezvous with Vanessa. Knowing that Ev wasn't stationed at the building, and didn't stay long, we would wait for him to leave so we could follow him. If luck was on our side the police wouldn't show up to move us along as we sat idling in a no stopping zone.

"When I asked Jimmy if he minded if I left the car behind the hotel for a bit longer," I said to Vanessa, "I asked him about the woman with blonde hair he saw loitering there on the day that Charlie was killed to see if he'd remembered anything else. He hadn't. But I was also thinking about the possibility that whoever the woman was, that she was there to set you up, so I asked Jimmy if the woman's accent sounded authentic—not that he's an expert or anything. He said it sounded authentic to him, but thinking about it now, he thinks her accent was Australian rather than New Zealand."

Vanessa just shook her head.

"As I say. Jimmy's no expert."

"So back to the drawing board. Not someone trying to set me up."

"And back to the possibility that this mystery woman was Charlie's killer—not that I'm going to waste my time worrying about that."

"I appreciate you helping me," Vanessa said, earnestly. "I'm sorry for interrupting your life. If I wasn't here, you'd be working on your new play today."

"I don't know." I shrugged. "How did your photographing the funeral go?"

She told me about someone surreptitiously watching the people arriving at the funeral, and added, "I recorded everyone but I missed a lot of faces because they were coming from all directions. I don't think the resolution of the video—not to mention the poor angles—will yield much to help me identify people. It might be good enough for your play though."

"I suppose it is what it is, as they say. I saw several people who were semi-regulars at the restaurant, dining with Charlie. I took some photos. I can't identify anybody by name but I was thinking that maybe the people in my theatre group might know a name or two. Dag's suggestion, that our next play focuses on Charlie's murder, gives me the perfect pretext to email out the images to my group and ask if anyone can put a name to any of the faces."

"Brilliant."

"No promises, but you never know. Maybe one or two of them will be a Who's Who of Halifax."

As we neared our car, having eventually come to the conclusion that Ev wasn't likely to be returning to the convention centre that day, I mentioned to Vanessa that I might head for Casey's after work and asked if she wanted to join me.

"I need to spend the time online—sorry. Casey's is the local watering hole, I gather."

"Yeah, I drop in there pretty much every night after work. … Does that make me sound like a loser?"

"No. Why should it?"

"Peggy, my ex, criticized me for going to Casey's so often. She wouldn't come with me after awhile. She said it was because she didn't want anyone to think she was a regular, like being a regular was synonymous with being a loser."

"I don't think that. My friends and I have a pub we go to. It's important for networking, socializing, and providing mutual support. … So what's Peggy up to now? Living her varied and exciting life?"

"She's in LA pursuing an acting career. Pretty successfully

too apparently."

"And is there an exciting new woman in your life?"

"No."

"What about the woman we passed the other night when we were walking?"

I was surprised at the reference to Stacey. "Why did you mention her?"

"I had the sense when you saw each other that there was something going on. Some weird tension."

"Was there? I don't know. We're just getting to know each other. She was on her way home from Casey's."

"And you like her?"

"Yes, but I haven't been to the pub in awhile and I wonder if she thinks it has something to do with her; that I'm avoiding her."

"I see. And now, because of me, she maybe thinks you have another woman in your life."

"That too. Well, on the positive side, I don't have to wait for her to find out how boring I am before she loses any interest in me."

"Oh …" Vanessa patted my arm in mock gesture of comfort. "So you'll see her tonight … what's her name?"

"Stacey. … And what about you," I said, "if you don't mind me asking?"

"You mean in the romance department?"

"Yes."

"I have a partner: an artist. The starving variety. We rent a space in a former factory. Enormous windows and great light. Oozes the glamour of destitution."

"So this trip on behalf of Katie's child is a financial sacrifice."

Vanessa shrugged. "It is what it is, as they say."

I was apprehensive as I worked my way between the people walking or standing in the aisle of Casey's.

The two tables routinely sequestered by my friends were almost full, but I spotted an open chair between a couple of people that I only knew vaguely. They were both speaking to people sitting beside them and barely noticed me.

My eyes went around the tables and I spotted three of my fellow members of The Other Theatre.

There was no sign of Stacey though. Not at first. I eventually spotted her, almost hidden behind a linebacker sized actor that I knew from university. She was conversing with a man sitting beside her.

I got a server's attention and ordered a drink.

I was soon in conversation myself. The guy to my right had turned and we began chatting. He was asking about Charlie, not surprisingly since he knew where I worked.

The person sitting on the other side of me got up, leaving her chair empty. I paid no particular attention. Nor did I pay heed when the chair was re-occupied, assuming the woman had returned.

"Are you going to ignore me stranger?" Stacey said.

Her voice caught me off guard. Stumbling over my words, I said, apologetically, "No … no … I didn't see you."

Stacey smiled. "I was just kidding. I wanted to say sorry for your loss."

I had to think about that one. "Oh, right, Thank you."

"Where's your cousin tonight? Has she gone back to New Zealand?"

"You know about her?"

"Lumina told me."

With those words, life, began to feel lighter. "She's still here for a bit." I knew there would be a time for admissions about my lies but it wouldn't be tonight.

"You should have brought her with you."

"She doesn't drink." I immediately chastised himself for

yet another lie to weigh me down. "And how have you been?"

"Fine. School's good. I guess you were at the funeral today."

"Yes. There were a lot of people there."

"What happened to Charlie Lawrence was a shocking thing. Have the police identified a suspect?"

"I don't know. He was killed in his suite—the penthouse. I don't know the motive. He had someone over for dinner so that person could have been the one who killed him. There was also a woman spotted behind the hotel that afternoon. She was standing beside the garage door that led to the underground where Charlie parked his car."

Stacey looked at me attentively, a puzzled expression on her face. "What day ... that was last Thursday wasn't it? Thursday afternoon?"

"Yes."

"Do you know what time the woman was there? Beside the garage door, you said."

"I was told it was close to 4:30. … Why?"

"And the woman? What did she look like?"

"I don't know her age. I was told she had red or blonde hair. An Australian accent."

"That was no suspect. That was me."

It was my turn to stare. Stacey had mid-length strawberry blonde hair and a smattering of light freckles. "It was you? Behind the hotel?"

"Yeah. I was there to loan you the Agnès Varda video I promised because I knew I wouldn't see you in here for awhile because of your cousin's visit. Lumina told me you used the back door at work so I waited there until 4:30 or so and then left. That's the time when Lumina said you started your shift so I assumed that I'd missed you."

"I always get there early. Closer to 4:00." My response was automatic. "The woman was wearing a trench coat apparently. That was you?"

"It must have been, since there was no one else there. I was wearing a long coat, sort of looks like an army surplus coat. It was cool that day and the coat has large pockets which can hold a DVD."

"Jimmy, the receiver, said he spoke to you ..."

"The older guy that came out for a smoke?"

"Yeah."

"I remember him."

"He said you covered your face when you talked to him."

"He was due west. The sun was in my eyes. You must have walked that way at that time of day."

"Of course. I should have thought ..." It was often so bright when I walked up the alley for my afternoon shift that I would avoid the blinding effect by keeping my eyes on the pavement in front of my feet.

I must have still looked confused because Stacey said, "I'm not sure if you believe me."

"No, no, I'm sure it was you. It's just that when Jimmy described the woman ... you ... he said that you had an Australian accent."

Stacey smiled. "Oh. He—Jimmy, I mean—said 'hello' and I automatically said 'good day'. You know, the way Australians say it: g'day. It just came out. Out of habit. I lived in Australia for the last four years after all."

"And how did you say that New Zealanders say hello, again?"

"Kia Ora. It's a casual greeting. It can be used for 'thank you' too so far as I know."

It was past midnight. Stacey and I were walking in the direction of her apartment.

"Kia ora. I'll have to try that on Vanessa."

"I think it's Maori."

"So it's Maoris in New Zealand. We took that in grade school but I can never remember whether it's Aborigines in Australia and Maoris in New Zealand or vice versa."

"It's a little more complicated than that. The Maori are a distinct people whereas the aborigines of Australia refers to a collective of many indigenous peoples."

"I should have figured that out on my own. Here we speak of Indigenous people, or Native people, or First Nations people, or Indians, and sometimes Aboriginal people. And all the terms encompass a wide group of tribes."

"I'm quite possibly wrong, but I think that one of the Aboriginal tribes in Australia are Maoris."

As we arrived at Stacey's building, she said, "Do you want to come up for a few minutes? As I said, I have a class at 8:00 in the morning so I can't stay up for long. It's already late for a Monday night. And we'll have to be quiet because my roommate will be sleeping?"

"Sure. If you're positive it's okay. I feel guilty for keeping you up."

"Ten minutes. Just to take a break from walking. I'd like to show you some photos of Australia."

Ten minutes became twenty after Stacey pulled out a second photo album for me to peruse.

"You should get some of these enlarged and framed," I said. "At least I would if I were you."

"I plan to. After I graduate and am settled in a place of my own. Hopefully, with a job and a few dollars of disposable income."

Stacey yawned and I noticed her glance at her phone; to check the time I assumed.

"I'm sorry," I said, standing. "I'm keeping you up."

"It's fine. I enjoyed having you here. Next time we should get an earlier start."

I was pleased by the reference to a next time.

We walked towards the door but stopped on the way. There was a large photograph propped up against the lamp on the end table nearest to the hallway. A person in the picture caught my eye. "Fraser's a good professor," I said, nodding towards the photo. The Fraser in question was a former professor of mine.

"Yes. In fact it's his class that I have tomorrow morning and you know what a stickler for punctuality he is."

"I remember."

Stacey picked up the photo and handed it to me. "A group of us from his class went to the diner for lunch last week. Somebody had the waiter take the picture and we all got copies. It was a birthday lunch for one of the men in our class and Fraser came along."

My eyes quickly slid over the faces of the students sitting around the table in the diner. They were all freshmen, in my old program, so no one I knew. Until ... I stopped at one face. It was ... I moved the photo under the illumination cast by the lamp on the table and bent over for a close-up look. The face was that of a young woman. Her hair was pulled back. She wore a bulky sweater that hid her figure. But there was no doubt about it. It was Windy-May Attwell."

"This woman," I said, holding the picture up so that Stacey could see who he was looking at. "I recognize her."

Stacey craned her neck to get a better look. "Oh yeah, Janet. Where do you know her from?"

I was about to answer but caught myself in time. How cruel it would be to mention that I knew the young woman as Charlie Lawrence's mistress. "I don't know, but I recognize her. Maybe I saw her in a play. I can check my old programs. I keep them from every play I attend. You said her name is Janet. Do you know her last name?"

"Winters."

"I'll have a quick look. Now I'm very curious."

I put the photo back in place on the end table. No wonder, I thought, that neither Vanessa nor I could find an online presence for Windy-May. She was living under an assumed name.

I wished that I could ply Stacey for more information about Janet, but it would likely sound strange. Like I had a romantic interest in her classmate.

"She's a first year student, like me," Stacey said as we resumed out trip to the front door, "only she's part-time. I'm surprised that you may have seen her in a play. I didn't get the impression that she'd done any acting. She's … she's … not very polished. I figured that this school was her first experience with acting."

"Then I must have seen her somewhere else. It's just one of those times when you see someone's face and you know you've come across them several times in the past. It bugs you not knowing from where."

"I know what it's like. It always drives me crazy. Could she have worked at the hotel where you work? I know that it's pretty upscale but she wears some very expensive clothes. Things that none of the rest of us can afford, so she likely comes from a wealthy family since she's too young to have been out working."

"That's probably where I've seen her."

At the door, we hugged good-bye.

It wasn't until I was out on the street that it occurred to me that Stacey hadn't given me the Agnès Varda DVD. I stifled the urge to go back upstairs thinking that she was already getting ready for bed, and not getting the DVD might be a fortuitous oversight if it led me back to Stacey's on another night.

"So this girl, that goes by the name of Janet, is in Stacey's class tomorrow morning," said Vanessa, not as a question but to affirm her understanding.

"Yes."

"And since you went to the same university and took the same degree program—you said—would I be correct to assume that you know where this class is held?"

"You're thinking that I could show up and talk to Windy-May?"

"No. I can't see you getting much there. She's living under an assumed name. I doubt that publicly outing her in front of her friends would endear you to her, not to mention the fact that it would be a scuzzy thing to do do."

"It would. And I wouldn't do that. I could follow her though."

"Maybe I should be the one to follow her. If you show up you won't be able to explain your presence—at least not to Stacey. What are you going to say to her: 'I can't talk now, I'm stalking the hot young babe you go to school with'?"

"Right. I'll have to tag along behind you since I'm the one who wants to interview Windy-May."

"It would be better to catch her when she's away from the university altogether. We could do what we did at the funeral: split up. You could sit in your mother's car near the student parking or the bus stop and I can follow her on foot."

"With your camera?"

"Of course."

"You know something just occurred to me. Stacey said that Windy-May is only a part-time student and, in a polite way, she also said that she's not much of an actor at this point."

"Not surprising."

"I wonder if Charlie Lawrence used his connections to get

her into uni. You know they get a lot of applicants for her program and part of the process involves an audition. If what Stacey said is true, that Win... Janet has no acting experience, then it's not likely that she could have gotten in by herself. Her affair with Charlie may have been about that; that plus tuition and clothes ... Anyway, there's something I was thinking about that I wanted to mention. Remember what Lumina told me she overheard Charlie say to Brian Hemmings? He said that it surprised him how well a certain 'she' was doing babysitting, but that he still wasn't going to give her the role she wanted because she can't act. I wonder now if he was talking about Janet and not his wife. I don't know if Charlie mentioned the babysitter's name or not. Lumina may have just assumed that he was talking about Addison because—in Lumina's view—Addison's the world's worst actress."

"Which would mean that Charlie was likely stringing Janet along with a promise of a good role in one of his plays if she babysat in her spare time."

"Yes. A quid pro quo. It may have been what they were fighting over and why she was shouting about lies."

Tuesday

We'd been driving for fifteen minutes. It was much easier following a car on a country road than it had been in Halifax, with its traffic signals.

Everything had gone well, thus far. Vanessa had no trouble finding a good spot outside Janet and Stacey's class to sit and wait.

Before we headed over to the university, Vanessa recalled that she'd been wearing Ellis's blonde wig the night that we passed Stacey in the street, so she went dressed as herself.

As the classroom was emptying, Stacey walked past her with no sign of recognition, and she had no trouble picking out Janet before falling into step behind her.

Vanessa said that she couldn't believe how young Janet appeared to be and would have pegged her as sixteen or so had I not indicated that her real age was more likely to be nineteen.

The secondary highway we were travelling along made it easy to stay well back of Janet's car—a late model Civic, of the sports variety—maintaining it as a dot in the distance.

My cell beeped so I checked it. It was an incoming text from Lumina. I opened it and read it out loud: "You may be right. I never heard Charlie mention the babysitter/actress's name. I just assumed it was Addison he was speaking about."

"News flash," Vanessa said. "Charlie Lawrence was a lying prick."

"Shocker. Didn't see that one coming. It doesn't suggest that Janet had anything to do with Charlie's murder though."

"No. In fact, it suggests the opposite. Not getting a role is not the sort of thing you kill someone about."

It was twenty minutes since we'd left Halifax behind. Spent mostly in silence.

I said, "It's only speculation that Janet may be looking

190

after Sam, or know where she is. I'm worried that I may have given you false hope."

"I understand, and it is speculation, but following her still makes sense, even if Sam isn't at her destination. You can speak to her and ask about Sam."

"We make a good detective team. Helping each other. … I just want you to know that if we don't find Sam this week, and you have to go home, that I'll keep looking for her."

We—by which I mean Vanessa—had found Janet Winters' Facebook page after I got home from Stacey's the night before. It was fairly sparse. Amid the seemingly requisite selfies was a photograph of her in camo, holding a rifle.

"This could be innocent," Vanessa said, "dress up, or maybe an actor trying out a character. Or a day hunting. I know what you're thinking, that the picture proves she's involved in a far right group."

"But in itself, it doesn't," I agreed.

"No, but maybe we need to be super careful to make sure that she doesn't see us following her, or make her suspicious about your motives if you get to speak to her. Those people will kill anyone who tries to out them—I mean, on the off chance that she is …"

Vanessa had also spent time looking for any reference to Janet online, on other sites like Parler, Truth Social, Twitter, 4chan, Reddit, Signal, and Gab. Others too whose names I don't recall. And she'd found nothing about Janet or Charlie Lawrence. She told me that, "In the work I did in the past I was accessing publicly available information, like stuff that came from the Paradise Papers that exposed corporations using off-shore vehicles to avoid taxes, like shell companies, captive insurance, and the rest of it. Stuff that was exposed because someone leaked data. But I see nothing here. Nothing linking Janet or Charlie Lawrence to any far right activity. Just public facade. This is a job for security experts and computer geniuses, not artists out to prove that commonly accessible information is being ignored, and that the wealthy are getting a free pass."

Stage Direction for the theatrical version of *Playing With Shadows.*
Image to be projected onto the stage screen.

We drove past a trailer park. Then a tiny subdivision of up-scale houses, fields, lone houses dotting both sides of the roads, and a few businesses.

"Look! She's turned right," Vanessa said.

I pressed down on the gas pedal, aggressively, since we would no longer appear in Janet's rearview mirror. I wanted to get close enough to keep her in view.

The country road that she'd taken turned out to be one of those that follows the lay of the land, with twists and turns that make it impossible to see very far ahead. It was my worst case scenario.

"I'll try to catch up to her," I said anxiously.

"We need to take a good look at any place we pass in case she turns into a driveway," Vanessa replied, leaning forward in her seat to study a prosperous looking house and grounds set well back from the road. A large SUV of some sort sat in the driveway. "Let's hope we spot Janet's car before we come to any other roads running off of this one."

We rounded a corner and I immediately slowed down in front of a dirt road or driveway on the left. There was a closed gate across it. The road beyond it disappeared into the bush.

Signs on each side of the gate announced that this was private property. A large, homemade placard attached to the gate screamed in all caps, NO TRESPASSING.

"And let's hope she hasn't gone down there," I said.

We'd just gotten back up to speed when we rounded a corner and saw a house on the right.

"There! There!" Vanessa announced triumphantly.

I saw what looked to be Janet's car parked beside a bungalow that was similar in size and character to a school portable.

I even caught a glimpse of Janet, from the side, as she was disappearing through the side door of the house.

I maintained my speed until we'd driven around another

corner, then pulled to the side of the road.

"I can make a three-point turn here," I said. "I don't see any way that we can watch the house from the car though. Even from that place." I nodded in the direction of the other side of the road. There was an overgrown driveway and a boarded up house of the same vintage as the one that Janet had just disappeared into. "I'd guess that we might be able to watch the road in front of Janet's house but that's about it."

"Right. That's fine if we're going to follow her. But aren't you going to approach her and ask for an interview."

"I am," I said with false conviction, nervous about the prospect.

"Great. While you're doing that I'll scout her house on foot. I see you have bug spray here, mine's back at the apartment. Let's hope there's no dog. Did you see any?"

"No, but then I didn't see much of anything. I was focused on Janet. How bout we rendezvous here after? If you discover there is a dog come back here immediately and wait. Otherwise, I'll likely be sitting here when you return—I mean depending on how I get on with Janet."

"Have you got your speech ready?"

"Yeah. Let's hope it works. If it doesn't, at least I'll get a close-up of the place."

"And let's also hope nothing bad happens."

Comforting words those.

Vanessa opened the car door and stepped out. Stepping onto the down slope of the ditch she liberally dosed herself with bug spray then lobbed the spray can back into the car.

I was glad to see that she sprayed her hair from the bugfest that she was undoubtedly headed for. In my experience, bugs were attracted to anything perfumed, like shampoo.

"Good luck," I said, as the door was closing.

I watched Vanessa carefully make her way through the ditch and muscle her way into the thick bush.

I turned the car around and headed for Janet's.

As I turned into the driveway I noticed a wooden sign dangling from a post in the front yard. It read, 'The Styles'.

Janet's Civic was still parked in the driveway and I pulled up behind it.

I took a deep stage breath and opened the car door.

Janet's smile instantly soured when she saw that it was me standing outside her door.

"What do you want?" she said aggressively while closing the door so that it only remained open about the width of her face. She'd clearly recognized me and I had the sense that she was wary of me as much as she was angry. It wasn't unexpected.

"I'm hoping that I can interview you for a play my theatre troupe is writing," I said, trying to make it sound as casual and friendly as possible.

My tone didn't seem to register since Janet's demeanour remained the same. "How'd you find me? Through something at Charlie Lawrence's no doubt."

I chose not to answer. I'd come with a prepared story about getting her address from someone I knew who worked at the university's registrar's office. It was just as well that I didn't have to use my lie since I didn't know if this was the address she'd given the school.

I plowed on with my mission. "I'm part of a theatre company, and we want to do a documentary play about the murder of Tanya Tucker and cover it from all sides. I'd like to interview you, as Windy-May—sympathetically. You won't have to provide us with a photo and your current identity won't be revealed."

Janet pushed her face into the narrow door opening then turned her head to look up the driveway, like maybe she was expecting someone. And maybe that person didn't know her true identity.

"How did you get my name?" she said, once again looking at me, but now glowering.

"I overheard Charlie say it one night last week in his suite. It's not a common one. That's about all I heard of your conversation and whatever it was about isn't germane to me." And then inspiration struck. "Of course, if you'd also like to participate in the play as the actress Janet Winters, you'd be welcome. It wouldn't pay much—if anything. But it would be a credit and some experience. It'll be a professional production; although a small one. All the people in my theatre company are graduates, now working in the industry."

If Janet was wondering how I knew that she was studying acting, the question didn't seem to concern her. It may have been that the lure of an acting job had pushed other thoughts away. "So, in that case, my actual identity would remain a secret?"

"Yes."

"I'll have to think about it." Her expression softened. "I'll speak to you. Come in." She stepped back and opened the door wide.

As I stepped forward I stole a glance towards the back of the house. There was no sign of a dog, pen, chain, or Vanessa.

In this scene, Peter and Janet will be in front of the stage screen while Vanessa's silhouette will be visible behind the screen as she looks about and through a window of the house.

Peter Russell

Where were you living at the time of Tanya Thomas's murder?

Windy-May Attwell

In Alberta. I'd gone there a few months before, after my mother left, to live with my dad's sister.

Peter Russell

Why did your father send you there?

Windy-May Attwell

He said it was because he was unable to look after me and I should live with a woman.

Peter Russell

Do you think that was the real reason?

Windy-May Attwell

I know what you're suggesting and I've wondered about that too; whether my father knew what he was about to do. And I think he did. A week after I went out west, Dad sold my mother's house to someone, so

shipping me out may also have been
motivated by money. I mean his lack of it.
Without me here he didn't need a house.
Funny thing, the house still sits empty ...
abandoned. I guess that whoever bought it
must have thought the land would be a good
investment for the future.

Peter Russell

Did you ever see signs of what your dad
was about to do?

Windy-May Attwell

Well I was young, but yes, definitely. He
had the same tropes he would say over and
over. Homophobic, misogynistic, racist
stuff mostly. He used to say that one day he
would kill one of those—you know, the 'n'
word—for taking over the country and
replacing white people; taking their jobs
and their country. He said a revolution was
coming. I live with the guilt of never having
said anything to anybody. But he was my
dad, you know, I refused to believe he
would ever do what he said and when I had
these twinges of discomfort, thinking that
he might follow through on his words, I felt
I owed him my loyalty to say nothing to
anyone.

Peter Russell

Besides guilt, how would you describe your
feelings after the murder?

Windy-May Attwell

When I first heard about the murder I was
appalled and didn't want to believe it was
true; that my dad was guilty. I usually stood
up for him afterwards, saying he was

innocent, but there were also times when I hated him for what he did. So I knew in my heart that he was guilty. I was angry at him too—in the selfish way a kid will be—not just for what he'd done to Tanya Thomas but because my friends turned away from me. I got called names and even got beaten up. I had to change schools and I was particularly sad about that because it was the first real school I'd ever gone to.

Peter Russell

You didn't go to school in Nova Scotia?

Windy-May Attwell

I went to my uncle's house every day, at my mother's insistence, and was home-schooled by my aunt and uncle along with my cousins. My mother was very religious —as was my aunt—and she wanted me to have what she called, a 'Christian education'.

Peter Russell

And what was that like?

Windy-May Attwell

Strict. To some degree I think we followed the provincial curriculum in subjects like Math but with some striking differences in other subjects.

Peter Russell

Such as?

Windy-May Attwell

Well there was no sex ed, unless you count being taught that abstinence is the only option, abortion is murder, and women are here on earth to procreate. Oh, and that men are head of the household. Science too, of course, was a little different.

Peter Russell

So no Science?

Windy-May Attwell

Oh no, we studied science and were told to respect it. We learned about plants and animals but we were taught that evolution was wrong, carbon dating was liberal nonsense, all races were not equal in God's eyes, and that dinosaurs lived at the same time as humans. Some things—like the argument that the science didn't support ideas about global warming—were based on politics not religion. Of course, what qualified as literature was highly selective. Same thing as history. Only certain parts of the curriculum were taught and from a particular perspective.

Peter Russell

Do you ever see your father now that you're back here?

Windy-May Attwell

No. I'll always be angry at him, I think. I'm haunted by my memories and want to press ahead with my own life. I no longer feel like I owe him anything. He destroyed both our lives.

Peter Russell

Besides socially, were their effects on you of what your father did?

Windy-May Attwell

Shame to the point of self-harm when I was young. Low self-esteem and dysfunctional relationships with men now, where I don't respect myself. I have a very strong desire to be a success in my field so that I'm not always known as my father's daughter.

Peter Russell

And, if I may ask, what are your politics?

Windy-May Attwell

I don't follow politics. So I'm neutral. An outcome of being a victim of politics maybe. Obviously, a lot of what my father used to say—all his prejudices and hate— are odious and I disagree with them. I suppose my biggest difference in views between us is that he thought that violence was a legitimate political tool. I don't.

Peter Russell

Why are you back in the province?

Windy-May Attwell

To pursue my dreams. I wanted to go to university and my aunt in Alberta couldn't afford it. My Nova Scotia aunt—my mother's sister—lets me stay here at her house for free. I work part-time at a couple of jobs for my family.

Peter Russell

Can I ask what sort of jobs?

Windy-May Attwell

This and that. Whatever needs to be done.

Peter Russell

On that subject, can I ask you about something that I heard Charlie Lawrence say? Something about looking after a little girl …

Windy-May Attwell

No. I don't want to talk about anything he said. I thought you only wanted to talk about my father.

Peter Russell

Well I do but this is important. If I can appeal to your …

Windy-May Attwell

No you can't. I think it's time for you to leave.

Vanessa walked out of the bush and scampered up the ditch as soon as I stopped the car in the spot where I'd dropped her off. She'd obviously been watching for me, under cover.

"How did it go?" I asked. "You okay?"

"Yeah. No dog, which was good. I walked right up to the house and got a close look at the backyard. There was no indication that there's been any kids around. How about you? I saw you got invited in. Saw the two of you talking."

"Yeah, Janet agreed to an interview. She even seemed friendly after awhile."

I'd been negotiating a three-point turn while I spoke. As we started up the road, we passed the rundown, boarded up house.

"I think," I said, slowing the car to look, "this might have been the house that Janet grew up in. She told me that after her mother died that her father immediately sold her mother's house and that it's sat, abandoned, ever since."

Vanessa studied the house and said uncertainly, "I suppose it could be the one."

"Well Janet's living with her aunt—her mother's sister— and the place is almost immediately across the road."

"So maybe the sisters bought the lots at the same time, thinking they could raise their families together sort of thing. It's sad, if that was the plan. There's a family where I grew up and the parents bought lots on their street for all of their kids."

"This road is about as desolate a spot as I could imagine. Why anyone would choose to live out here is beyond me."

"And did you find out anything about Sam?"

I felt bad, having heard the obvious note of hope in Vanessa's voice. "I'm sorry. I tried to ask but as soon as I tried to switch the topic of discussion to something Charlie said, she got annoyed and cut me off. Said she had only agreed to talk about her father's case and told me to leave."

We were nearing the edge of the city when Vanessa handed my cell phone back to me after listening to the recording of my interview with Janet Winters.

"She sounds sincere," Vanessa said, looking my way.

"Disarmingly open even."

"Funny she opened up so readily to a stranger; that she could be so trusting. Maybe it's evidence of the limited experience she's had of the world. Sounds like she's lived a fairly isolated existence."

"Ready to be exploited. Taken advantage of."

Vanessa didn't immediately respond. I suspected she thought that I was being overly solicitous to the point of refusing to see Janet as anything but a victim when it came to Charlie; the sympathy that men muster up with young women. But I may have been wrong because Vanessa eventually indicated that her thoughts were on other matters, when she said, "Thinking about it, Janet doesn't sound like she has far right attitudes."

"No. She hates politics. Not surprisingly."

"And I never felt like she was lying or trying to cover anything up. So, on the face of it, it seems unlikely that she and Charlie were tied up in some far right activity."

With chagrin, I said, "I guess it was always a pretty speculative leap to think that. Silly even. And not something that concerns me. … So what now?"

"I'd like to watch Janet and follow her. See if she goes to Sam."

"Watch her from where?"

"From the abandoned house across the road."

"You can't see her place from there."

"But you can see the road in front of it and I'll know if she leaves. If you don't mind, once we get back to your place, I'd like to take the car and drive back up here."

"Of course."

We drove.

"Maybe I'll head straight to the hotel," I said when we got to Halifax. "We're filling up with people arriving for the political convention that starts tomorrow and the day shift can use some help. I can get some overtime pay. I now need to take all the overtime I can get. So I can jump out when we get to the hotel and you can take the car."

"Sounds good."

Rather than drive around back, to the staff entrance, I planned to pull to the side of the road and stop just beyond the hotel. I'd get out and Vanessa would take the car.

I was watching the back end of a huge black SUV as we snaked our way along, and it struck me that it was similar to the one belonging to Ev Junior, when I suddenly woke up. "Is that Ev's car?" I said.

Vanessa sat up and leaned forward. "It is! I remember the license plate number."

We were directly in front of the hotel and, just as he had done the day before, Ev made a left and headed down the ramp to the convention centre's underground parking. I continued on past.

"What are you doing?" Vanessa said. "Why didn't you follow him down? Turn around.."

"I didn't think we could sneak in behind him," I explained. "And even if we managed the door, he'd see us."

"Which is fine. I've decided that, fuck it, I'm going to talk to him instead of following."

I made a couple of turns. I hadn't even come to a stop in the space in front of Charlie Lawrence's private garage door, when Vanessa exited the car and began to run down the alley.

I turned off the car, got out, and ran after her.

We circled the hotel until we were directly across from the convention centre.

With me following, Vanessa waded into the street, causing horns to beep and car breaks to squeal.

I pretended I didn't hear any of it and avoided making eye contact with any of the angry drivers as we scurried across the road and into the centre.

The security guard who reads Sartre obviously recognized Vanessa and smiled broadly when he spotted her striding up to the desk.

"I need to speak to Everett Collins immediately," Vanessa said. "I just saw him drive into the parking garage so I know he's here. It's a matter of urgency."

"Oh. Of course," said the guard. The smile left his face and his tone shifted to all business in response to Vanessa's commands. He picked up the handset of the landline telephone on the desk and punched in some numbers while leaning back in his desk chair, perhaps subconsciously, to back away from an anxious Vanessa who by then was hunched over him, her hands on the desk.

I heard the guy confirming with whoever was on the other end that Ev was on site and then asking that person to tell Ev that someone was waiting for him in the lobby who wished to speak to him.

"About his daughter," Vanessa prompted. "And it's urgent."

"It's about his daughter … urgently." There was a pause while the person on the end of the line was apparently speaking to Ev.

"Okay, thanks," said the guard, into the phone. Hanging up, he looked at Vanessa, "Mr. Collins will be right up. If you could please wait over there." He pointed to a couch and chair in the lobby.

The guy looked relieved and sat forward in his chair the moment Vanessa straightened up and strode towards the waiting area. Once there, she stopped and stood beside the coach, rather than sit, so I followed suit.

Ev, looking decidedly serious, soon stepped off the elevator.

"Vanessa!" he said, approaching her. "What's up? Is Sam okay?"

"I don't know know. Sorry for alarming you when I said I was here to see you about Sam. I said it was urgent that I speak to you because I've been trying to contact you for two weeks—I promised Bob and Letty that I'd check on Sam when I was here—but I've been getting the run around from your father."

Ev seemed to relax but still appeared to be puzzled. "My father?"

"I went to see him. He told me to go back to New Zealand. And that he didn't know where you or Sam were."

"Please, sit down," Ev said, pointing to the couch and chair. "This is all news to me." He self-consciously looked over his shoulder at the security guard who was doing his best to appear oblivious to what was going on. Or maybe to put on a show that he was hard at work while the boss was nearby.

Ev also glanced at me, and Vanessa noticed. "My friend, Peter," she said.

Ev and I shook hands.

When we were all seated, Ev said to Vanessa, "I knew you were in town. One of the security men at Charlie Lawrence's soiree told me that he saw you out on the patio and I ordered them to hunt you down." A statement accompanied by a smile. "I wanted to see you but they had no luck."

"They did actually. And they made me leave."

"Leave? Why would they do that?"

"I assume they were carrying out you father's wishes."

Ev shook his head. "I'm sorry … I had no idea. You said that Letty and Bob wanted you to check on Sam?"

"I did. They're concerned. They don't have an email or physical address to send anything to Sam or even a phone number. They feel like they've been shut our of their granddaughter's life. They don't deserve that."

"No they don't." Ev's sympathy seemed genuine.

"Do *you* see Sam?" Vanessa asked.

"I do, at my dad's." And a fleeting smile crossed Ev's face at the thought. "But I admit, not as much as I should."

"So you know where she's staying?"

"Dad said a couple of weeks ago or so that she's now staying with friends of his who have kids—girls—so she can be home-schooled with them. He'll take her on holidays and in the summer."

"Do you know where?"

"I don't think he said."

"And when you saw Sam does she seem okay?"

"More or less. She's quiet. But she lost her mother not that long ago and is in a new country with complete strangers so I assume it's not surprising. She'll adjust now that she has some other girls to be friends with."

I wondered if it was possible that Sam was more than a little unhappy but wasn't communicating it. Or perhaps she was being coached to say otherwise.

Ev glanced at his phone and I saw an example of what Vanessa had described. He seemed to love his daughter but didn't even know where she was staying and was too distracted by a phone call to dwell on her. "I'm really sorry about this," he said to Vanessa, and signalled his desire to wrap up their conversation with, "Do you have a phone number I can reach you at?"

"I'll give you mine I said."

Ev took a pen and small notebook from the pocket of his suit jacket and jotted down the number I gave him.

"I'll speak to my father and make sure you get to see Sam. I know she'll be happy to see you."

After Vanessa thanked Ev, I mentioned to him that she would need to see Sam soon since she was leaving on the coming Tuesday.

Vanessa confirmed what I'd said.

"Definitely by the weekend then," Ev replied, getting to his feet.

It was easy to get caught up with work and forget everything else. Like the old maxim says, time goes by faster when you're busy. The hotel was crowded with guests, in town for the national political convention of one of the major opposition political parties. They were meeting to elect a new leader and there was lots of buzz around town about it. The current party in power was hugely unpopular so whoever was elected in the next few days had a good chance of being our next prime minister. Current money was on a young woman named Anna Luce. She was an environmentalist and, if elected, would be our first openly gay and first mixed race prime minister.

The restaurant was packed, so much so that my deficiencies as a server were becoming self-evident. I wasn't used to covering several tables so found myself forgetting who it was that had asked for the glass of water or a clean fork, or who was still waiting for their bill or to have their order taken.

In spite of all of it, the frantic pace and the overcrowding, my thoughts kept drifting back to Vanessa, especially when I managed to take a look outside and saw it growing darker. In spite of Ev's promise to let her see Sam, Vanessa had still been determined to follow Janet. She said that she thought that Senior might talk Ev out of his promise and was convinced that Janet knew where Sam was.

Vanessa had told me that she also intended to have a look inside the boarded up house during daylight which meant that, if she was still there, she'd be sitting in my mother's car, hidden behind a derelict house, watching.

I worried that her approach would be too bold. I hadn't fully convinced myself that Janet wasn't connected to some far right cabal, although I agreed with Vanessa that my suspicion did sound alarmist and fantastic. But, I thought, if I was right, Vanessa could be in grave danger nosing around.

Lumina and I literally ran into each other in the kitchen at one point and I used the opportunity to ask her if she was going to Casey's that night.

"Of course," she said. "Are you?"

"No. My cousin is only here for a few more days and I won't be able to make it. Can you tell Stacey, if she's there, that I'll be back into my routine next Tuesday."

Lumina didn't bother to ask why I wanted Stacey to know my schedule. She just nodded, said, "Sure," and was back off, hustling to the dining room.

I watched her leave and recalled that she hadn't been at Charlie's funeral. Surprising, but not something I was particularly wanting to know the reason for. Seeing her reminded me that I still had some photos taken at the funeral that I needed to email to my fellow members of The Other Theatre hoping to attach names to faces.

I took a necessary break. Five minutes only, I told myself as I stepped out the back door, just to clear my head.

Jeremy was standing on the top step of the metal stairs, just beyond the door, smoking a joint. "Whew," he said when he saw me, "what a madhouse in there. Needed a break too eh?"

"Yeah," I agreed. "I'm not used to this." I caught myself before I could go any further. It was a habit I'd developed. Most of my fellow servers had seemed to be resentful that I was Charlie's sole waiter so I came to avoid any mention of it when speaking to them.

"I guess you saw the CCTV photos the cops released of Charlie's car, eh?"

"Ah, no. I haven't heard anything about that. Photos of Charlie's car?"

"Yeah, well you know how it's missing. It was supposed to be in Charlie's underground parking space but it wasn't. Somebody took it the night he was killed. Anyway, the cops put CCTV photos up online today. You see Charlie's Porsche driving past the hotel. There's pics from the front and back. And there's one from the side that was obviously taken by a camera on the outside of the new convention centre cus you can see the front of the hotel in the background. That's the one where you can see the woman driving the car. The cops are hoping that someone can identify her."

"And did you?"

"No. It's a woman with light hair … wait …" Jeremy tossed what was left of his joint and went to work on his cell phone which he'd been holding in his other hand. "Here." He handed me the phone.

You could see the woman fairly well, at least in some respects. Her face was bathed in the light of a streetlamp. She was shot from the side but her head was turned, looking directly at the camera, almost like she wanted to be seen. She had light coloured hair and, despite the night, sunglasses.

I suppressed my reaction. Hemmed and hawed a bit as if I was being unsuccessful in my attempt to identify the driver.

As I handed the phone back to Jeremy, I stole a glance at his face as if I needed to reassure myself that he wouldn't be thinking the same thing as me. He wasn't an actor, hadn't gone to school with me, was never seen at Casey's, and didn't know my friends.

"Recognize her?" Jeremy asked.

"No. I wish it was a better image. It's not super clear so it's hard to make out precise features."

I hadn't lied, not about the quality of the image at any rate. The photograph wasn't of sufficient definition that you could positively identify the driver of the car. But I'd lied about something else. The woman in the photograph appeared to be my roommate Ellis. Vanessa perhaps, in her disguise, but more likely Ellis. It certainly wasn't Janet Winters or Addison Lawrence.

The panic I suddenly felt was because the woman in the photograph, in all likelihood, was the person who had murdered Charlie Lawrence.

I wondered if Lumina had seen the photo. If she, or anyone else in my group, felt that the woman in the photograph resembled Ellis, would they report it to the cops?

Of course they would.

But it couldn't be Ellis in the photo, I told myself. It was the wig that Vanessa had been wearing all over the place that put it in mind that this was Ellis. The woman in the photo could have been wearing the same wig.

I gathered up my phone and went to the washroom. From the Facebook page of the local police I downloaded the photo that Jeremy had just showed me. I then texted it to Ellis along with a message that read: 'Didn't know it was you who bumped off my boss. LOL'. I was certain of a humorous response that would assure me that the woman in the picture wasn't her.

Stage Direction for the theatrical version of *Playing With Shadows*.

Image to be projected onto the stage screen.

215

I was immediately apprehensive when I turned onto my street.

Because it was so busy at work I'd managed to suppress my concerns about Vanessa being out in the country, following Janet Winters, but now there was no holding them back. I felt a rush of anxiety at the thought that she wouldn't be at the apartment when I got home and I began to consider what I would do if that was the case.

As I made my way up the walk in front of the house I spotted Mrs. Tate sitting at her front window. It struck me that she was now on guard, every night, and well past her bedtime. It occurred to me that she was only there when I was out. As soon as I was home I would hear the crunches that told me she was walking about and then there was silence for the rest of the night. She wasn't nosy. She was protecting Vanessa.

Mrs. Tate nodded in my direction. Would wonders never cease.

I glanced up and saw a light in the front room of my apartment and was buoyed by the fact that Vanessa was back from her mission.

As I climbed the stairs it occurred to me that I didn't know who Mrs. Tate was on the lookout for. Was it the goons or was it the cops? Or both. Perhaps Vanessa had told her that the police appeared to regard her as a person of interest.

I wondered if I should call the police detective, Ryder, to tell him it had been Stacey hanging out at the back of the hotel, and not Vanessa. I wasn't thrilled with the idea. I didn't want him bugging Stacey. Plus I realized that it would be pointless to call. The woman in the CCTV image I'd seen bore a resemblance to Vanessa. That alone would be reason enough for the cops to continue looking for her. It was possible that the photo had always been the reason they were focused on her (although how they would know the woman in the photo looked like Vanessa was a mystery).

When I stepped through my apartment door I saw Vanessa sitting behind her laptop and felt another rush of relief. It's a selfish thought I know, but I didn't want to again feel the high level of anxiety that I'd experienced earlier in the week.

"Sam is definitely not being looked after by Janet," Vanessa said, "at least not at her place. Her and the aunt were at home all evening and it was only them."

"And she didn't go anywhere?" I asked.

"Nope. Neither of them."

"Maybe in the daytime," I offered. The two of us were sitting in my small living room, in our usual spots, nursing glasses of wine. "Maybe we could watch her house beginning first thing in the morning. I could come with you."

"You're on. Oh, and you're right. The abandoned house belonged to Janet … I mean, Windy-May's mother. There's a sign, exactly like the one across the road that says 'The Styles', only this one says 'The Attwells'. Oh, and the Attwell sign looks like it was run over by a truck, the wooden post that supported it is snapped in half."

"Seems like the two sisters were close. Copied each other."

"It does. I'm guessing the Styles' sister had a family too because her sign says 'Styles', in the plural."

"Um."

"Oh yeah, I looked all around the old Attwell place by the way. I pried some boards away from the back door, just enough to get inside. It's pretty run down but it looks to be in good enough shape that it could be fixed up. Strange that someone would just abandon it like that."

"Oh, I have something to show you." While I was retrieving a photograph on my phone I said, "The cops released some CCTV photos today, looking for help to identifying the person driving Charlie Lawrence's stolen car the night he was killed. The police post said the picture was taken at 11:00 PM, so I think that the person in it may be the one who killed Charlie."

"And then left in his car."

"Uh huh." I handed Vanessa my phone and waited.

She sat upright and leaned into the phone to study it. "Any ideas who it is?" she asked.

"No. It looks like my roommate Ellis, but I know it's not."

After further study, Vanessa said, "I can see why you're saying that. She could be wearing the wig in her room, which I gather is modelled on her hair …"

"It is."

"But her face isn't clear. I suppose it even looks like me when I'm wearing the wig and sunglasses … hmm."

I was grateful that Vanessa had simply taken me at my word, that the woman in the photo wasn't Ellis. And she was even trying to bolster the idea that one shouldn't conclude as much. "I sent a text to Ellis with the photo attached," I told her.

"What did she say?"

"She hasn't replied. Busy with her play, I guess. Plus she isn't a phone person. The battery on hers is always dying. And she keeps inadvertently turning on silent mode. … Were you wearing the wig the night of the murder?" I asked abruptly.

"What? Oh, yes, I see what you're getting at. I did have it on. So no one stole it and returned it."

I felt embarrassed that I'd asked the question but it had to be considered.

I went through my phone and uploaded all of the photos from Charlie's funeral that captured faces of people who I recollected having been at the restaurant as his guests. I cropped them to include only the face of the person I recognized so there'd be no question about who I was asking about when I emailed the collection out to my theatre group.

I included a note that said: "Can anyone help me identify who these men are? They're all people who I recall dining with Charlie at the restaurant. This could be valuable information if the subject of our next play involves getting reactions to Charlie's murder."

Stage Direction for the theatrical version of *Playing With Shadows*.

Image to be projected onto the stage screen.

Wednesday.

It was going on for noon and Janet Winters was still at home. Her aunt had departed first thing in the morning, in her red sub-compact.

Vanessa and I were parked on the property of the boarded up house that she'd looked into the day before. I agreed with her. Up close, it looked like it could be made livable. The siding seemed fine. The windows were boarded up but the frames weren't ancient. Creepy vibe though.

We'd positioned ourselves behind a broken down shed at the end of the property closest to the Styles house. From there we could watch the end of Janet's driveway with no chance of being seen by traffic going in either direction.

I glanced at my phone. Still lots of time till I had to go to work. It occurred to me that if things dragged on here that Vanessa and I would have to leave. By tagging along I was a liability, limiting her ability to follow Janet's car should she not leave until later in the day.

I felt Vanessa's nudge to my ribs. I looked up to see Janet's Civic pulling onto the road.

I started my mother's car and looked at Vanessa.

"Long enough," she said.

Having given Janet a sufficient head start we headed off in pursuit.

"There she is," I said. It had only taken thirty seconds or so to get close enough to bring Janet's car into view.

I slowed down to maintain the distance between us.

We saw the brake lights ahead go on and watched the Civic turn into the driveway of the expensive house up the road.

I didn't immediately alter my speed, unsure of what to do. It didn't take long before we passed the house. Janet had parked behind the black SUV we'd seen parked there each time we passed the house and we saw her walking up the driveway.

Immediately after passing the house I slowed and, once we were out of sight of the place I pulled to the side of the road.

"Well we now know where the aunt was off to," Vanessa said.

The woman's red sub-compact was also parked in the driveway of the big house, beside the black SUV.

Vanessa had twisted around in her seat, and was bobbing her head to and fro, hoping to get a glimpse of the house.

"I'm getting out," she said. "I want to see what's going on." Without waiting for a response, she exited the car and crossed the road.

I shut off the motor and followed suit, hustling to catch up.

Vanessa led us into the bush and then veered left until we got to the perimeter that bordered the lawn of the house. A huge expanse, neatly trimmed, perhaps an acre in size. We stopped when the house came into view and stood under cover of the trees.

We heard voices before we saw anything. Then a door slammed. Soon people began to appear behind the house. Janet, in the company of two girls, maybe twelve years old. The three of them were engaged in lively conversation.

Behind them a small girl emerged from behind the house. She wore pink rubber boots.

Vanessa started and clutched my arm. "Sam!"

I watched Sam wander across the end of the driveway, moving in our general direction. But, on reaching lawn, she turned and went in the direction of the road.

A man's voice could be heard. It was loud but I couldn't tell what he was saying. Janet stopped and looked over her shoulder. She then turned and walked back towards the house while the two girls she was with drifted off in the direction opposite to us.

I saw Sam skip for no reason, the way small kids do, then bend and pick up what looked to be a small stick. By then, Vanessa was running across the lawn in Sam's direction.

I hesitated, not knowing what to do, before turning and running in the other direction, back to the car. I turned it around, drove to the house, and parked in the driveway behind Janet's car.

Off to my right I spotted Vanessa. She was kneeling and talking to Sam so I stayed in the car and watched, leaving the two of them alone.

"Sam squealed when she saw me," Vanessa told me later, "and ran to hug me. I told her that I'd come to see how she was. She just kind of gushed, rapid fire, saying how much she missed me and her grandparents. Said she missed home and didn't like it where she was. Luckily the house blocked us from view so after Sam calmed down we had a bit of a conversation. I gathered she was really excited about going into Halifax tomorrow. She's going to present some flowers to a woman tomorrow. Somewhere in the city. And she'd been practising where to not touch the stems. I think she was excited about the whole thing because they'd told her she would get her picture in the paper. But that was as far as we got before Janet came around the corner of the house, saw us, and began yelling at me to keep away from Sam. I don't know if she knew who I was and had been warned to keep me away from Sam or if she thought I was a stranger, maybe a kidnapper, and was touching a child she was supposed to be supervising during lunch break."

I got out of the car and headed toward Vanessa and Sam as soon as I saw Janet striding across the lawn. We arrived at Vanessa's side at the same moment.

Vanessa was still kneeling when Janet grabbed her shoulder and tried to pull her away from Sam yelling, "I told you to keep away from her."

Vanessa stood and pushed away Janet's hand, saying things along the lines of, "I'm her mother's best friend. I came to see her."

Janet again yelled at Vanessa to keep away—it seemed her go-to response to things she objected to. At full volume. Janet grasped Sam's shoulder and tried to pull her away but the little girl responded by throwing her arms around Vanessa's legs.

All the noise had apparently attracted the attention of the older man who I saw step around the corner of the house. But he immediately retreated.

"Let her explain," I said to Janet.

"You! You!" she said, still at top volume, directing her words to me, "What are you doing here? Oh don't tell me, you're the friend of Stacey's who told her you recognized me. So all of the stuff about doing a play about George was a lie, you were just trying to find Sam to kidnap her."

"No, if you will listen ..." but that was as far as I got before I heard the old man barking something about getting off his property. Everyone turned in his direction. He was a couple of metres behind us, holding a rifle at his shoulder, and pointing it in our general direction.

Vanessa knelt down and said to Sam, "I have to go now," and with the volume of her voice increasing, loud enough to ensure the old man got the message, added, "but I'll be back to get you soon, I promise."

Janet knelt and wrapped her arms around Sam who twisted and turned and tried to break free.

Vanessa got up and strode off towards the car.

"And don't come back," the man said.

I stood looking at him, weighing my options, then walked off after Vanessa.

As I backed our car out of the driveway, Vanessa commanded, "Don't go too far away, I want to call Ev." Her anger soon gave way to frustration and tears before I was two hundred metres up the road.

"I'll head back to that church, just along the main road, that we pass on our way here." And figuring that Vanessa would need a few minutes before she phoned, I added, "We can sit in the parking lot and you can phone from there."

Ev was on speakerphone and angry. "I can't believe he'd point a rifle at you. With Sam there too! He was always a humourless authoritarian when I went to school there, terrifying us kids with stories of eternal damnation if we didn't obey. But the rifle? He's gone off the deep end."

Vanessa asked, "What's his name?"

"It says 'Hutchinson' on the sign," I said.

Ev said, "Yes. I called Senior today to ask about Sam and when he told me she was at Hutchinson's with a couple of his granddaughters I felt sick at the thought of being the one responsible for subjecting her to that. The only thing that made the experience semi-bearable for me was that it was his wife who did most of the schooling. He's a businessman but taught at least one subject a day."

"I didn't see the wife," Vanessa said.

"No, she died a year or two ago. Maybe that's what's pushed him round the bend."

The was a pause where no one said anything.

Vanessa and I were sitting in the front seat of my mother's car, which faced the road running between Hutchinson's and Halifax. During the conversation I'd kept a watch on the road. It was a quiet stretch and judging by the tire skid tracks on the pavement it was the spot where young locals came to burn rubber on Saturday nights. Confirmation of its isolation.

Eventually Ev said, "So, is Sam still at the house?"

"We're about a kilometre away and no one has driven past," I said.

"Okay then, I'll call Senior and get permission to let … No, I'll drive up there and take you over to Hutchinson's myself. Where are you?"

I began to explain but Ev cut me short saying that he knew the place I was talking about.

Vanessa felt somewhat better, I think, after we'd spoken to Ev, especially since he seemed to have found his courage. But we sat in silence.

She eventually picked up my phone and I gathered that she was signing on to the internet. "You don't happen to know Hutchinson's first name, do you?" she asked.

"I do. There's a sign in the yard, same as the sisters' signs, that says 'Glenn Hutchinson' on it."

Vanessa went to work on my phone, while I continued to examine every car that went past. I assumed that if Sam was being taken out of Vanessa's reach that it would be in one of the three cars that had been in Hutchinson's driveway. I saw none of them.

"I think I found him," Vanessa said, "or at least some things about him. He's described as an Investor. He comes up as a big supporter of an anti-abortion group. Likes to pose for their website photos handing over cheques for what I assume to be for significant amounts,"

"Sounds like I would have imagined him."

"I know this organization, it's big in the States. They get a lot of donations from some really deep pocketed types. They have large rallies. Lots of far right militia guys attend them."

"They pay them for protection?"

"Oh no. They invite them—unofficially of course, so they can disavow any connection—and the men show up."

"Why would they invite them?"

"To add a bunch of bodies and loud voices, plus make the groups more visible. Normalize their presence."

"But why would far right militias attend?"

"For the same reasons, plus they're anti-abortion too. It's part of the great replacement theory that white people are being replaced by immigrants and Jews. They want white Christian women to procreate and increase the white population. These far right guys actually want white women to be forced to have children."

"And Hutchinson supports them. And he's teaching Sam. No wonder Ev was pissed off when he heard where she was staying."

"Yeah. Supporting this anti-abortion group is one of the

ways that these so-called respectable businessmen and businesses sponsor far right militia events without doing so directly."

I took my eyes off the road to look at Vanessa. "Meaning that respectable, Investor Glenn Hutchinson, is connected to the militant, anti-state, far right."

"You got it."

I picked up my phone off the seat where Vanessa had set it.

A text from Ellis had arrived, in reply to the photo I'd sent her taken the night of Charlie Lawrence's murder. It read, "LOL. Looks more like Jeff Weird in his wig than me."

I replied, "Jeff has a wig too?"

She answered, "Yeah. Two were made for the play. He gave me one and kept the other. He was wearing it at the after party as a joke. Looked just like this woman."

I didn't instantly reply. I had the feeling you get when you have a piece of a jigsaw in hand and you know it will mark a breakthrough, only you don't know where it goes.

A follow up text from Ellis arrived while I was advising Vanessa of what she'd written. "I was just joking. I can't see Jeffie as a murderer. It does look like him though."

"Know anything about his politics?" I texted back.

She replied, "No, but he must be fairly liberal since he's involved in the planning of a performance at the convention tomorrow."

I handed the phone to Vanessa to read the text exchange as Ev's SUV pulled into the church lot and pulled up beside us.

Soon, Jeff Weir was put on the back burner.

Having decided to take both cars, I followed Ev's SUV onto the Hutchinson's driveway and parked behind him. None of the three vehicles that had been there earlier remained.

We walked together to the front door, with Ev in the lead. He pressed the door bell and we waited.

After getting no response, he pressed again.

"I'm going to look around back," Ev said.

When the three of us got to the empty yard, Ev knocked on the back door. He tried the knob. It was locked. Vanessa and I went to every window. We knocked loudly and called 'hello!'. It was pointless. They'd gone and taken Sam with them.

"Damn!" Vanessa lamented after we all came together back at the front door. "Where could they have gone."

"They didn't take the road to Halifax," I said. "I watched it the whole time we were at the church."

"Maybe they went to the sister's place up the road," Ev said.

"The sister?" said Vanessa.

"The Styles?" I ventured, looking at Ev.

"You know it." He was visibly surprised. "Mrs. Styles and Mrs. Hutchinson were sisters. Denise and Donna. My father told me that Mrs. Styles was the one now teaching the kids, along with the old man of course, and with relief from her niece ..."

"Windy-May Attwell," Vanessa said.

"Right. The two of you seem to know a lot. Her mother was Belinda, the third sister. Anyway they may have gone up the road."

"Let's go," said Vanessa.

"I know where it is," I told Ev, as a way of indicating that, since I was parked behind him that I would take the lead.

We piled into our respective vehicles. I didn't think that Sam was in any danger but I still raced along the road, with abandon, desperate from the thought that if we didn't catch up to her that she might disappear once again.

The Styles' driveway was empty but I drove up it, parking by the side door. Ev stopped his SUV behind me.

The house appeared to be deserted but we followed the same procedure we'd employed up the road. We banged on the doors, peered through the windows, knocked on them, and called 'hello!'.

When we regrouped by the side door, Vanessa asked Ev if there was anywhere else he could think of that the group might have gone.

He said 'no'.

"At the old Attwell place maybe?" Vanessa asked.

"I can't see that," replied Ev, but the thought apparently suggested something to him. "They could be at the old farm."

"Where's that?"

"We passed it. Well, I mean we passed the gate to it back there."

"That's a farm?" I said, surprised. "It looks deserted."

"Oh it is, but it's not boarded up. The owner and his friends hunt around there. We used to hear the rifles going off all the time."

"Whose the owner?" Vanessa asked.

"The brother of the three sisters. The couple who lived there bought building lots for their three daughters and left the farm to the son in their will. He's never been a farmer though. He works in the city, in theatre."

"Jeff Weir," I said automatically.

"I see you know that too. Anyway, they could have taken Sam there."

"Then let's go," said Vanessa.

"The gate has a padlock on it," I said.

"We could park at the old Attwell house," said Ev. "It's a two minute walk across the old field to the farm from there. I know the way. I grew up around here."

As we once again, got back into our cars I recalled that first dinner I served Charlie Lawrence in his private box. His guest was Jeff Weir; the one who I'd heard say, "She's fucking hot. I can hook you up with her no problem." It was shortly after that, that I began serving Charlie's dinners with Windy-May in his suite. It struck me as likely that, in addition to all his other wonderful attributes, that Jeff was not above pimping out his own niece.

We left our cars at the old Attwell place and began trudging, with Ev in the lead, first through a swath of bush, and then along a path that ran parallel to more bush. An overgrown hay field was on our right.

I noticed three wooden frames standing in the field, with targets painted on them. A firing range.

"It's just up here," Ev told us—presumably speaking about the farm buildings. At that exact moment we heard multiple cars starting up. "Dammit," he said, and began to run as best he could on the rough trail.

Vanessa and I followed suit. The group with Sam must have been watching for us to drive past the entrance to the farm before leaving, I thought.

We didn't make it. By the time the farmhouse and driveway came into view the cars were gone.

"We need to go back. Get our cars," Vanessa said, "and urgently!"

We all turned around. But at that moment a man stepped out of the bush to block our way. He was three metres away and pointing a rifle at us. Goon #1!

We turned back towards the farm buildings, instinctively looking for a way out, despite the presence of the rifle, but two other men stepped out of the bush to close off that direction. A very large man and goon #2, also holding a rifle and pointing it at us.

I breathed a sigh of relief. The big man was the cop who'd come to my apartment. I was about to say his name, Ryder, when Ev said, "Rex! What are you doing here?"

"Just stand still," the large man replied.

We were marched along the path which ended behind the old barn.

On the way, Ev asked Rex what was going on and was told, "You'll find out soon enough."

229

We were ordered into the barn. It was empty, for the most part. Wisps of straw here and there. At one end was what looked like a cross between a science lab and a distillery.

We—the three prisoners—stood and looked about the building.

"Where's Sam?" Ev asked Rex.

"Well she's not here," answered one of the goons and then laughed. The other goon followed suit.

"Sit down on the floor," Rex said to Vanessa. "Your back to the beam." He pointed to one of the beams that supported the hay loft.

"Don't do anything!" Ev said to her. "What the hell is going on Rex? There's going to be hell to pay when my father hears about this."

"We just need you all to stay here for awhile," said Rex.

Goon #1 walked over to Vanessa, grabbed one of her arms, and kicked her feet out from under her.

Ev lunged towards them but goon #2 raised his rifle and pointed in at his head. "I'll shoot you Ev!" he yelled. Ev stopped.

"Sit up against the post like you were told," goon #1 commanded Vanessa. Rex had retrieved a roll of duct tape from somewhere and handed it to the goon. Vanessa's arms were forced back, and her wrists bound together behind the post.

The procedure was repeated with Ev who was tied to the next post. "Does my father know you're doing this?" he asked Rex.

"Nope. And he ain't gonna ever know," goon #1 said.

"Shut up!" Rex told him. "I'm sorry Ev," he added in a softer tone." He turned towards the goons and instructed them to tie me up. "I'll call the boss," he added and walked out of the barn.

The goons watched him go. "And we all know what the boss will say," goon #1 said to the other.

"The boss killed Charlie Lawrence didn't he?" It was out of my mouth before I had a chance to think. Both goons turned in my direction.

"Good for you," said Goon #2. "Charlie boy made the

mistake of refusing a financial donation towards the lab and the weapons. Even threatened to go to the cops when he heard that the plan had changed." His tone was an aggrieved whine, like Charlie had brought things on himself.

"Shut the fuck up," #1 said. Then, to me, he sneered, "I know who you are. And I remember what you did."

"Me too," chimed in #2.

Both goons moved towards me, rifles brandished. "You're the tough guy who likes to smash people with rocks." And, with that, he raised his rifle and hammered me in the head with the rifle butt.

I fell to the floor and instinctively covered my head. Vanessa screamed. I was jolted by a second blow. A kick maybe. As I was losing consciousness I heard Rex yelling, barking the words, "Syd!" and "Wally!"

Stage Direction for the theatrical version of *Playing With Shadows*.

To be played out on the stage in front of the screen.

*Two men are sitting at a dinner table and
can be heard laughing. A telephone rings.*

Charlie Lawrence

Just a second Brian. Let me grab this.

Brian Hemmings

Not a problem Charlie.

Charlie Lawrence

(Speaking into the phone) Yeah, hi. Thanks
for getting back to me.

Jeff Weir

(audible but indiscernible words)

Charlie Lawrence

I'm having dinner with Brian but it's okay.
I'll keep it brief.

Jeff Weir

(audible but indiscernible words)

Charlie Lawrence

I wanted to ask you to help us find our
friend Vanessa.

Jeff Weir

(audible but indiscernible words)

Charlie Lawrence

No. We did have her address. Senior followed her home from my soiree. But then Syd and that other clown tried to scare her back to New Zealand. Like that's going to work. So, to no one's surprise, as soon as she realized we know where she lives, she fucked off.

Jeff Weir

(audible but indiscernible words)

Charlie Lawrence

She'll surface soon enough. In the long run I think the best plan is still to play the waiting game. I never agreed with Senior's crackpot scheme to intimidate her. She's gonna keep harassing us. The only way to win is to wait till she runs out of money and has no other option but to go home. Better yet, if she doesn't go home on her own, to wait until she's overstayed and then report her. She'll never get back into Canada after that.

Jeff Weir

(audible but indiscernible words)

Charlie Lawrence

Well, she doesn't have any friends, so far as I know, unless you count the guy with the rock at my soiree.

Jeff Weir

(audible but indiscernible words)

Charlie Lawrence

He did. Maybe he's a hero and has given her a place to stay.

Jeff Weir

(audible but indiscernible words)

Charlie Lawrence

Well that's a problem. The place only has cameras in the ballroom. We just went with what was there. Vanessa was out on the terrace so no telling who she was with. She and the hero guy might have snuck in together. We only discovered she was at the soiree cus Syd spotted her outside.

Jeff Weir

(audible but indiscernible words)

Charlie Lawrence

Absolutely. I was going to ask.

Jeff Weir

(audible but indiscernible words)

Charlie Lawrence

We're assuming she met someone out on the terrace since she has no friends in Halifax—she's only been here a few weeks after all.
So first thing the guys did was to watch the CCTV and take screen captures of all the men who went outside. They're trying to match them to the invitations but they aren't getting anywhere. Problem is that Tweedledee and Tweedledum know fuck all.
I'd like you to go in and help them—if you would. You know everybody who was at the soiree; more than me at any rate. Plus a bunch of people who got invites are friends of yours and I wouldn't know them from Adam. Can you go in and give them a hand?

Jeff Weir
(audible but indiscernible words)

Charlie Lawrence
Right, right. Of course, if the guy snuck in with Vanessa we'll never know who he is but we won't know if that's the case unless we eliminate everyone who we know wasn't involved first.

235

Stage Direction for the theatrical version of *Playing With Shadows*.

To be played out *behind* the stage screen this time.

Two men are sitting at a dinner table

Brian Hemmings

Is Senior still worried about the Kiwi broad nosing around?

Charlie Lawrence

Yeah, but Brian, there's no way she's ever gonna find the kid.

Brian Hemmings

I don't understand Charlie. Why doesn't he just let her say 'hi' to the girl? It's not like it will hurt anything. Maybe once she sees that the kid's okay she goes back home.

Charlie Lawrence

That's what I told him but he seems to think that she—Vanessa, I mean—is looking into his business practices and personal life … and mine.

Stage Direction: Telephone rings.

Charlie Lawrence

Jeff. What's up?

Jeff Weir (on phone)

(audible but indiscernible words)

Charlie Lawrence

No, no, it's okay. Just having dinner with Brian. We were talking about Senior ... and keeping the kid from Vanessa. Here, let me put you on speakerphone. Okay, go ahead.

Jeff Weir

I wanted to bring you up to date. I got together with Syd late last night after my show and had a look at the CCTV screen captures from the soiree. He'd narrowed it down to a couple of possible guys as the one who rescued Vanessa. I went through the invitations. I tossed almost all of them since I knew what those people looked like. And then I found it! There was an invitation that I'd sent to an actress whose name is Ellis. Well I knew Ellis hadn't been at the party because she's on tour so, ergo, someone else had used her invitation.

I dropped Ellis off at her place after rehearsal one night when she was performing in one of my plays and she mentioned having a roommate. I can't remember his name but it was a man. My guess was that this roommate had used her invitation and was one of the two unknown faces on the video.

Syd and Wally went over to Ellis's place first thing this morning. My instructions were that, if they saw Vanessa, they weren't to approach her but just to see if she was there. They parked in front of Ellis's house and watched for a few hours. Syd called in eventually and said that there was no sign of Vanessa but that they'd seen a woman with blonde hair come out at ... like nine in the morning.

The boys thought the woman they saw must

have been Ellis. They don't now her so they were just guessing but I'd told them what she looked like before they left. The woman they saw matched Ellis's description but it couldn't have been her since she's away.

I wondered if it was another blonde. Or maybe Ellis had come back. Then I remembered something. Ellis shaved her head for the part in my play cus she played a woman getting chemo and we got a couple of blonde wigs for the early scenes. We gave her one when the show was done. Maybe, just maybe, I thought, this blonde broad was really Vanessa.

So I jumped in my car and drove to the house. After I talked to the boys I sent them away and stayed there. I have a pretty good idea of what Vanessa looks like from Ev's description, but she doesn't know me. Anyway, so I'm sitting there and watching, and guess who comes sauntering up?

Charlie Lawrence

Vanessa in a blonde wig.

Jeff Weir

Close. It was her—I'm sure—but she wasn't wearing the wig.

Charlie Lawrence

Tell me you didn't approach her.

Jeff Weir

I didn't approach her. I had nothing to say.

Charlie Lawrence

Good, good. Have you talked to Ev?

Jeff Weir

No, I left that for you. I know the plan is to keep them apart. So you gonna tell him?

Charlie Lawrence

Hell no. It's better he doesn't know. They're buddies apparently, according to Senior. I think we should let her be. I just want to keep tabs on her.

Jeff Weir

Do you think she's looking into your affairs?

Charlie Lawrence

Let her. I have nothing to hide.

Jeff Weir

I don't want it to come out about our connection. I mean about my niece and our plan.

Charlie Lawrence

Don't worry about it. How could she know?

239

I came to, laying on the floor of the barn. Disoriented. Couldn't understand where I was. Or why I felt like I did. My head was pounding, unbelievably so. I tried to move and pain shot through my temples and eyes.

I wanted desperately to close my eyes but forced them to stay open.

Looking about, I saw Vanessa and Ev. Recalled that their wrists had been taped behind them. Around the posts. I spotted Rex over in the lab. No goons in sight.

I tried unsuccessfully to sit up. Realized that my hands were taped. But unlike Vanessa and Ev, mine were wrapped around a post in front of me. Probably because I'd been prone on the ground and couldn't sit up when I was bound.

"You okay Peter?" Vanessa said in a loud whisper.

I mumbled something.

"Do you know where you are?"

"Yes," I managed. "That guy's the one who came to my house." I nodded in Rex's direction. The movement made me dizzy. "Said he was a cop." Looking at Ev, I added, "Does he work for your dad?"

"Sort of," Ev said. "He's a chemical engineer. My dad hired him as a consultant to advise him on chemical weapons and how to counteract them."

"Is your father involved in this?"

On cue, Rex lumbered into view, stopping in front of us. I hadn't seen him approaching. "Welcome back Sunshine," he said in my direction. "And, in answer to your question. Mr. Collins has no idea about our little mission so he's not going to rescue you. And he'll ever shop us to the cops. We've got too much on him, plus he knows what will happen if he does. And anyway, he's loyal."

"That's quite a lab you have there," I said.

Ryder looked at the lab like he was seeing it for the first time. "The bare minimum. But even that takes a considerable amount of money."

"Is that a chemical lab?" Vanessa asked.

"Perceptive of you."

"Where's the boss and your goon buddies?"

Rex snorted. "I'm sorry none of them could be here. The boss will come later. He had an event he couldn't miss. A one time performance he's directing at the convention centre." And he laughed.

"Syd and Wally are part of the security team at the convention centre ..." said, Ev, his voice trailing off. He appeared to have been thinking out loud rather than informing us of the fact.

I saw the alarm on Vanessa's face. She was definitely a few steps ahead of me. I was still preoccupied with the intense pain in my head. "Sam said that she'd be presenting a bouquet of flowers to a woman. Is that where? What's going on there?"

"Ah, so the nosy bitch knows nothing about what's going down," Rex taunted. "We were scared you might, but you know nothing. That's because we don't shoot out mouths off like other idiots. We have no social media presence, only dispense information on a need to know basis, and exercise military style discipline. Your little friend is going to meet Anna Luce, the shining star of the radical lesbian left. Well, it won't be long before we see that star flicker out—after she gets her flowers."

"You're going to kill her with whatever poison you're manufacturing," Ev said with certainty.

"With a nerve agent, yes," said the big man.

Vanessa interjected, "Sam told me that she wasn't to touch a certain part of the flower stems." The full horrifying import of what she was saying was on her face. "You're going to poison Anna Luce with the flowers."

"Good for you," mocked Rex.

Ev struggled against his restraints, pulling and yanking with all his might, grunting like an enraged animal.

"And what about Sam?" asked Vanessa, clearly horrified. "She'll be in intense danger."

"Quiet," Rex boomed. "Both of you, shut up. If she ends up having a little, let's call it an 'accident' afterwards, well all wars have collateral damage."

"Collateral damage!" Vanessa yelled. "She's a little girl! You can't justify that!"

"I don't need to justify anything, not to you at any rate." Rex took a deep breath and continued in a quieter tone. "I hate your type, making your name by snooping into the business of others." His face had reddened and he was clearly angry. But he quickly calmed down. "I guess I can tell you what's going on. It's not like you'll be around for long; long enough to tell anyone. The little girl is a mongrel, half native, a Maori. Ev's old man disgraced himself taking her in. She's disposable. She's the enemy who needs to be gotten rid of. We need to reclaim our country, take it back from all the groups who have dominated it: the Jews, feminists, trans-whatevers, Blacks. We need to restore the wealth and power of white people. Take it back from radical left politicians like Anna Luce. Restore freedom."

"You're one sick fuck!" I blurted.

"Sick? No," Rex replied evenly. His tone said that, in his mind, he was a teacher lecturing some recalcitrant youths. "We're patriots. But now my dears, sadly I must leave you. Unless I miss my guess there'll be permanent resting spots for all of you up the road, beside Belinda, once the boys get back with the boss."

And he shuffled out of the barn.

Stage Direction for the theatrical version of *Playing With Shadows*.

Image to be projected onto the stage screen.

"Peter," Ev said. "Can you stand up?"

"I could try," I replied.

"If you manage it, I can tell you how to get free. Easily. It's something my father showed me. An old security move that works with duct tape. First though, you have to stand up and press yourself against the support post."

With a fair bit of effort I got myself onto my knees and 'walked' on them until my belly was against the pole. "My wrists are bound pretty tight," I told Ev."

"All the better."

I managed to hoist myself up, enough to get my right knee up, the sole of my shoe planted on the floor. As I began to rise I felt a rush of nausea. I hesitated, then eased myself back down.

"You're doing good," Ev assured me.

I braced myself for what was to come. For maybe fifteen seconds. Then, in one effort, I lurched upward until I was standing. If I hadn't been restrained I'd have fallen over due to dizziness, but I remained upright.

"Get yourself stabilized," Ev coached.

I stood quietly, acclimatizing myself, until the worst of the dizziness passed. A full minute I think. "Okay," I said.

"Now I know you're probably thinking that you can't break free from the tape, but you can because your hands are in front of you. But it's going to take all your strength. Are you ready?"

"I am."

"Good. Alright. Push yourself against the post and raise your hands as high as you can while keeping your wrists together."

I obeyed, forcing my hands above my head. I kept my wrists together—not that I had any choice in that.

"Peter, when I say 'now' I need you to pull your hands down as quickly as you can and force your elbows wide apart."

I doubted Ev's plan would work but psyched myself for what was to come.

"Now!" Ev said.

I brought my hands down as fast as possible while forcing my elbows apart.

Vanessa and Ev ran along the path beside the field.

Still dizzy, I more or less staggered behind, slowing us down.

Our cars sat where we'd left them, behind the old house. Out of sight from the road. But the glove boxes were open. All identifying papers were gone. VIN tags removed no doubt. Cell phones missing. Radios smashed. Presumably, both vehicles were eady to be burnt.

George Attwell's wife was buried somewhere near here, I now knew. Had his daughter known?

I told myself that there was no damn way that this would be my final resting place too.

"C'mon baby," Ev said to the SUV. We held our collective breath. Had the motor been tampered with? The vehicle started right up.

And we were off. Flying over the roads. Breaking any number of safety laws.

No one spoke.

I rested my head on the car door, positioned so I could watch the oncoming traffic. Even the slightest bounce sent blasts of pain bouncing around my skull, forcing me to sit up to watch.

I was hoping that we wouldn't pass anyone returning to the farm because it would signal that Jeff Weir and the goons had accomplished what they'd planned to do.

The curb in front of the convention centre was taken up by three or four black limos. I caught a glimpse of Anna Luce on the sidewalk. A crowd surrounding her. A movable group making its way towards the front door of the hotel.

"We're not late!" Vanessa said triumphantly.

The crowd of people watching Anna Luce had been moved away from the front doors of the convention centre. In both directions. The two groups of people, sporting signs and hats, were cheering. Their cell phones were out, taking photos and videos.

Ev nudged his car through the crowd at the head of the garage ramp. One of the two driveway guards bent his head to look into the SUV, saw who was inside, and nodded. He waved at his partner who stepped out of our way.

We quickly descended the ramp into the building. Ev sped towards the elevator. Once there, we jumped out of the car, leaving it running. Vanessa pressed the elevator 'up' button. And we waited. An excruciating twenty seconds or so while Ev cursed.

Exiting at the main floor, Ev sprinted ahead while Vanessa and I tried to keep up.

Ev was stopped at the entrance to the centre's floor. Two beefy bouncer types sporting vests that said 'Security' were blocking the doorway.

"Sorry sir, you have to have party credentials to enter the floor," I heard a guard say as Vanessa and I arrived on the scene. Ev began to yell at the men in protest.

I looked about. We'd just passed a set of stairs and I knew where it led. I'd been here before, with Dag.

"C'mon," I said to Vanessa, tugging at her sleeve. The guard at the steps—one of Ev's guys—had been watching his boss's dispute. A pushing match was now underway. The guard rushed to Ev's side.

Vanessa and I ran up the stairs. The door at the top was unlocked. We stepped inside the sound booth and I locked the door behind us.

Dag, sitting at a sound board, spun in his desk chair. A look of surprise crossed his face. "Peter!" he said.

Vanessa rushed across the booth to the window overlooking the floor. "There's Sam!" she said, "At the side of the stage with Janet."

Joining Vanessa at the window I saw that Sam was holding a bouquet of flowers. Janet Winters was standing behind her with a hand on Sam's shoulder.

Anna Luce could be seen working her way down the centre aisle between the temporary seating. A shuffling procession. Luce was smiling broadly. Waving to people. Touching fists with others. Exchanging banter.

"You can't be here …" Dag said. Not for the first time. But I'd been tuning him out. "Peter …" It was a frustrated plea.

"It's life or death Dag," I said.

He threw up his hands in disbelief.

"No really. There's a plan to kill Anna Luce by the people on the stage."

Dag stepped up to the glass. Anna Luce was almost at the stage.

"We need the PA system," I said. "We need you to kill the music. Give Vanessa a mic and let her talk."

Dag was watching the floor but now looked at Vanessa. Like he was seeing her for the first time. And then he moved into action.

I saw people looking up at our window when the music was killed.

Dag grabbed the mic perched on a table. Handed it to Vanessa. Flicked it on and said "Go ahead."

"Quiet please," Vanessa said into the mic.

Anna Luce's procession was in front of the steps to the stage. They didn't respond.

"Stop!" Vanessa commanded. The procession halted. Heads turned to look up at the booth. Anna Luce's included.

"There's a little girl on the stage." Vanessa said. "She has flowers. She doesn't know that they're coated with sarin or some sort of nerve agent meant for Anna Luce."

Confusion followed. Anna Luce was immediately surrounded. I heard some shrieks. I saw numerous people in the crowd heading for the front doors.

At that moment, someone began pounding on the door of the sound booth. Yelling to be let in.

"Sam," Vanessa said into the mic. "It's Vanessa, sweetie. Listen to me. Throw the flowers you have onto the stage, right in front of you. Then keep away from them."

Sam looked our way. She saw Vanessa pressed to the window.

"Do it now!" Vanessa said.

Janet took hold of Sam's shoulders, and began pulling her offstage.

Sam tossed the flowers onto the stage, still looking at Vanessa.

"Good girl," Vanessa said.

Janet stopped dragging Sam away from the flowers. She began pushing her towards them.

A woman blocked their way, holding up her hands. Janet pushed against her but others bolstered the line of defence.

And that's when I saw him, Jeff Weir, sprinting up a side aisle. Forcing his way through the current of people moving away from the stage.

And there was a second figure. This one on the opposite side of the room. He was doing the same thing.

Jeff made it onto the stage. He rushed to the flower bouquet. Picked it up. He moved across the stage. Towards Anna Luce.

He was almost there when Ev came from the other side of the stage. He threw himself at Jeff's knees and tackled him. They ended in a heap on the floor.

Ev stood up. Then backed away.

Jeff Weir lay on the stage on top of the flowers.

I'm told that he began to convulse and reach for his throat as if he was strangling.

Ev approached him and turned him over, He kicked the flowers away then knelt beside Jeff. And he looked up at the booth.

Vanessa again spoke into the mic. She asked that if there were any doctors in the room that they proceed to the stage. And she told them to keep away from the flowers.

Stage Direction for the theatrical version of *Playing With Shadows*.
Image to be projected onto the stage screen.

The goons were located hiding in the abandoned Attwell home after a two day manhunt. They'd apparently been backstage at the convention centre with some of the nerve agent to be put on Sam's hands after she'd delivered her flowers to Anna Luce. Just enough to kill her within an hour or so, to make it believable that she'd come into contact with some of the substance from the bouquet, but not so much that she couldn't have walked offstage.

For the late Jeff Weir and his cabal, Sam's life was entirely expendable. In fact, their safety required it.

Janet told the police that the poisoned bouquet had been delivered to the suite at The Alexander Graham Bell Hotel that they'd secured to prepare Sam for the event. If the flowers were sabotaged, she knew nothing about it.

A minuscule amount of the substance that was found in the suite, however, proved that this was where the flowers had been treated with the nerve agent. Based on that conclusion and the testimony from Sam about her training, Windy-May Attwell was charged with the attempted murder of Anna Luce. So too were her aunt and uncle.

Rex, the engineer and murder planner, was located driving across Quebec and returned to Nova Scotia where he was charged with a long list of offences.

After Belinda Attwell's body was recovered, George Attwell was charged with her murder.

Ev interceded with Senior, taking charge by all accounts. Deciding to do the right thing—at last.

Rex had told us that Senior had a past with the plotters and wouldn't turn them in if their plan had succeeded.

That would have been enough for Ev but Senior had also sent Sam to live at the home of Glenn Hutchinson, undoubtedly knowing who he was. Ev decided to never let his father have any decision making powers over his daughter ever again. Or even to see her.

Tuesday. We all gathered at the airport for Vanessa's send off, and Sam's, whose destination was her grandparents' place in New Zealand.

Windy-May had promised Sam that she'd be in the news if she delivered the flowers to Anna Luce and Sam had been excited at the prospect. And there was no disappointing her.

I watched her walk through the airport with her dad. People were pointing at her in recognition. Some waved. Her beaming face was on the front page of the papers in a newspaper box. She was thrilled. The young want attention. No shadows for them.

Sam passed through security on her own.

She was met by a waiting woman who'd passed through the same gate, unobtrusively, fifteen minutes earlier. A woman in a trench coat, sporting the blonde wig and sunglasses she'd just put on. A shadow woman.

I remember the media video I'd seen of the interview with George Attwell talking about the murder of Tanya Thomas. In it, Attwell said how well he'd scouted the security before the slaying. He knew all about it. When to time his visit. When the guard would be away. Where the security cameras were. He even knew about the empty upstairs office upstairs and that it would be unlocked. I wondered if Attwell had been pressed about how he'd known all these details. I took a walk after reading the story, to the Maclean-Dill Building, and sure enough, the guard at the front desk was sporting the logo of Collins Security.

Two weeks after the attempt on the life of Anna Luce, Ev Senior was charged for his involvement in the Tanya Thomas murder.

I suspect that Jeff Weir would only have used Sam in his attempt to murder Anna Luce because he was secure in the thought that Senior would support his version of events afterwards. And not just because Senior would think that he might be implicated if he didn't go along with Jeff's story of knowing nothing about the poisoned flowers, but because Jeff knew about his involvement in the Thomas murder.

Once again I was walking Stacey home after Casey's last call.

We were swapping stories about the best advice we'd come across regarding writing scripts for theatre or film.

Stacey was interested in the use of silence. "A lot of times you don't need dialogue; body and eye movement will do," Stacey said. "Like at the end of *The Graduate*. The two young people have run away and we see them sitting on a bus. Shot from head on. They don't speak. They look afraid and confused. We're left to read their minds."

"Hmm," I said. "Makes me think of a scene from the film *Brooklyn*; screenplay by Nick Hornby. We see a young couple, also in a bus, shot head on. The boy asks the girl for a date and she accepts. They both play it cool but immediately look away. And break into big smiles. Whew! … I guess if there's a lesson there about writing, it's that you never treat a scene as throw away. In the scene, it's clear that they have both spent the week thinking about this moment. When the guy begins to ask the woman to dinner he starts to play out a dialogue. He's thought the whole thing through. And when she accepts it's obvious that she too has played out her answer all week. It tells us how young and inexperienced the couple is."

"And how much they like each other."

"Yes."

I hadn't meant the story to be about me. Or me and Stacey. We were hardly a pair of innocents. In the quiet that followed I winced at the thought that Stacey might think I was employing such a heavy-handed approach to incline her to say yes when I asked her out.

It was Stacey who picked up the conversation. "I'm still finding it hard to believe that Janet—I mean Windy-May Attwell—was involved in what happened. I thought she was genuinely sweet. Naive."

"Sweet she isn't. How badly damaged must she have been to be able to believe at the age of thirteen that her mother's killing was deserved for threatening to expose her father's plans. According to what they're now saying on the news, the mother was the only one not in on the Thomas murder."

"Maybe she's a better actress than I gave her credit for. She already knows how to act to some degree. She must have known that most people would find her views repulsive, so she kept them to herself."

"People may have shunned her if they knew she was George's daughter."

"That's true too," Stacey agreed.

"Vanessa was talking to a detective yesterday—a real one—and he told her that the plan had been to humiliate Anna Luce. Charlie was involved in that plot along with Jeff Weir and his clan. Apparently, it was only when Charlie was approached by Jeff, for money, that he heard about the poisoning. He threatened to go to the police and was killed to stop him."

"So Charlie had some scruples after all."

"Yes. Not many, but he had a line he wouldn't cross."

"And Jeff Weir was a murderer."

"Yes. In all likelihood, he was also the mastermind behind the murders of Tanya Thomas and his sister Belinda. It was him who bought her property from George. Maybe pressured him. … Plus he was a stalker and pimp on top of everything else. … Windy-May underwent years of grooming. I feel sorry for her in a way. You should have seen the inside of Jeff's farmhouse—Vanessa snuck in and took some pictures yesterday. There were Confederate flags on the walls. A bunch of others. Some I didn't know. One of them is apparently called the Schwarze Sonne. Other flags were obviously SS, Neo-Nazi, and KKK. There was white supremacy and hate graffiti everywhere. Stuff attacking liberal politicians, women, and especially Jews."

"A completely sick environment."

"Yes."

When we reached Stacey's apartment she leaned heavily

against me. Wrapped an arm around one of mine. Then invited me upstairs, "To get the Agnès Varda DVD."

Now I don't want to appear presumptuous or neurotic but I had a feeling that this was the end of one story about me and the start of another.

BY 2.0. (License link: https://creativecommons.org/licenses/by/2.0/)
https://www.flickr.com/photos/cobraverde/3774872641/

page 165: Quote from:

Nancy MacLean

<u>Democracy In Chains: The Deep History of the Radical Right's Stealth Plan for America</u>. Viking. New York, NY. 2017

Image from: Marco Bianchetti. Public Domain.
https://unsplash.com/photos/HY5r718ee7U

page 192: Piotr Wilk. Public Domain.
https://unsplash.com/photos/KfXWIkOk4hI

page 211: Monica Silva. Public Domain.
https://unsplash.com/photos/2o3HrdMUkJg

page 215: Gabriel Gurrola. Public Domain.
https://unsplash.com/photos/u6BPMXgURuI

page 219: Skitterphoto. Public Domain.
https://pixabay.com/photos/little-girl-walking-shadow-wall-2176130/

page 243: Thom Milkovic. Public Domain.
https://unsplash.com/photos/o79oTCONaJw

page 249: Maksim Istomin. Public Domain. (Crop)
https://unsplash.com/photos/N8VVveiNVbU